OUTSPOKEN LOVE

Jeri Stockdale

ISBN: 978-1-956654-36-3

CHAPTER 1

Seattle, Washington, September 1910

The rain slowed to a mist as Anna Bailey stepped off the streetcar, her pulse quickening as she hurried to the post office gripping the precious women's magazine article she'd worked on for weeks. *Why do women still have such little say? We have no vote, our ideas are often brushed aside, and even in publishing our words are not seen as equal to a man's.* Eleven submissions. And eleven rejections. This time would be different.

As she dodged mud puddles, horse-drawn carriages, and a few motorcars on the cobblestone street, loud angry words brought her to a quick stop. Ruby, her dearest friend, stood toe-to-toe with a large intimidating man who hovered over her small frame. A few curious onlookers watched, but did nothing. Anna rushed to Ruby's side, ignoring the wetness seeping into her patent leather boots.

"Who do you think you are?" The large man's raised voice reverberated around them. "Work comes first. You don't see *me* missing any days, do you?"

"No, Mr. Morgan, sir, but my child was sick, and I had no one—"

"Excuses. My restaurant needs reliable employees. Besides, a woman has no business being a head cook anyway."

Anna stiffened. Memories of humiliation, and the blatant way her former headmaster had treated her differently because she was *only a woman* came flooding back. Even though she had been at the top of her class, Mr. Hargrove made sure she did not receive the college scholarship she needed to realize her dream of a journalism degree. Queasiness engulfed her like a tidal wave. And when Mr. Morgan turned toward his carriage to leave, the desperation on Ruby's face prompted Anna to step in.

"Excuse me, sir."

The man stared, eyebrows knit together, and Anna's stomach churned.

"Please sir, give her another chance," Anna pleaded. "She needs this job. Her husband is a fisherman. He has been gone six months without sending any word."

She waited by Ruby's side. *Please God, soften this harsh man for Ruby's sake.*

"If my businesses were run according to all the hard luck stories I hear, most of which are not true, they would fail." He turned his attention back to Ruby. "You're fired. You hear me? Fired!"

Anna exhaled the breath she'd been holding. *Another unanswered prayer.*

Ruby grabbed onto his coat sleeve as he tried to enter his carriage. "Please Mr. Morgan. I really need this job."

He shook her off like a pesky fly and Ruby lost her balance. Anna tried to catch her, but Ruby fell, toppling Anna to the ground. They landed in the rain puddle with a splash, and a jolt hard enough to send Anna's wide-brimmed hat with its blue satin bow flying. Remembering her manuscript, she stiffened as she saw her precious pages floating on the water, scattered outside the mailing envelope she had not yet sealed. She reached for one of the sheets, but her dirty hands only smeared more mud, blotting out the text. Her hard work was all for naught.

"See here, Morgan." An attractive man in a business suit stepped forward and Morgan gave him a hostile glare. Morgan didn't answer, but instead seated himself in his carriage, yelled at his horse and driver, and smirked as they drove away.

The brown-haired man's eyes narrowed, and face darkened as he watched Morgan's departure. As he slowly turned his attention to her and Ruby, his features softened, and he held out his hand. "Allow me to offer my assistance."

First, he lifted Ruby to her feet. She struggled to pin up the auburn hair that had tumbled from its coif onto her shoulders. Meanwhile, he helped Anna as well. He had a gentle touch, his dark brown eyes shining, with what? Admiration? He let go of her hand after a long moment, retrieved her rumpled limp hat, and bent down to retrieve the mud-splattered pages.

Anna gathered as many as she could also, but quickly realized it was a lost cause. Weeks of work down the drain. *I'll never make the article deadline now.*

He reached into his breast pocket and gave her his handkerchief.

"Thank you," she said, as she attempted to wipe the mud off her hands.

"Are you all right?"

"Yes, I am. Just angry." She noticed the compassion etched on his face. "Look at my manuscript. Absolutely ruined."

"You're a writer?"

"Yes, just not a published one. Yet." Anna liked the quirky smile he gave her in return. She glanced at Ruby. "Oh, Ruby, what will you do?"

Ruby shook her head. "He was an awful employer, but at least I could pay my bills."

The kind gentleman took out his wallet and fumbled through the contents, growing more flustered by the minute. "I was going to give you my card, but I seem to have lost it. I'm Daniel Wright."

"*The* Daniel Wright, the reporter for the Seattle Post Intelligencer?" Anna smiled and tried to tone down the excitement bubbling up inside.

"Yes, guilty as charged." He stuck his hands in his pockets, jingling their contents, a smile playing around his lips. He glanced at her, at the ground, and then back at her again.

She liked the way the gold flecks in his brown

eyes twinkled when he smiled. Then, with a jolt, she realized she was studying him. "I am sorry. My name is Anna Bailey and this is my good friend, Ruby Olson."

They both dipped a small curtsey in their mud-stained ankle-length skirts.

He nodded as he touched the brim of his hat. "I'm happy to meet you both. If there is anything I can ever do for either of you, please feel free to call on me at the paper."

Anna and Daniel gazed at one another again, until he reached for his pocket watch and checked the time. "Oh no. I'm late. Excuse me ladies, I have a pressing appointment."

"Yes. Certainly. Thank you for your help," Anna said.

"Yes," Ruby added. "We appreciate what you did."

Daniel nodded again and left at a brisk pace.

He seems too good to be true, just like another I remember. Anna pushed those thoughts aside. Daniel glanced back three times as he hurried away.

"Well, what do you know?" Ruby said, smirking.

Anna looked at her friend. "What?"

"Who would have thought my most unfortunate day could turn into one of *great* fortune for you."

"What?" Anna repeated.

"Didn't you see the way he was watching you?"

"I do not know what you are talking about."

"Oh yes you do. We're as bedraggled as half-drowned wharf rats, which he didn't even seem to notice."

"You have an overactive imagination." Anna shook her head. "I still cannot believe your boss was so unkind as to fire you. We need to do something to stop men like him from treating us so unfairly."

"We certainly do." Ruby reached into her embroidered handbag. She pulled out a flyer and handed it to her. "Here."

Women's Club Meeting, Open to new members. Join us for lunch at 1:00 p.m., Monday, September 15th, at the home of Dr. and Esther Thompson, 225 Sixth Avenue W. The discussion topic will be "The Women's Suffrage Movement, How You Can Make a Difference."

"Will you come with me?" Ruby asked.

"I am not sure what I think about the movement. It's certainly controversial." Anna gripped her muddy manuscript tighter. Then her stomach rumbled. "Let's go. I have no need to go to the post office now, and I will go to the market at Pike's Place another day. At the least, we will get lunch, and maybe we *can* make a difference."

Anna put her soaked pages in her empty market bag, with new determination in her soul. "Besides, bullies like Morgan shouldn't be allowed to get away with such despicable behavior."

And yet, why do men like him seem to? She watched thunderclouds forming across the expansive gray sky. *God, another question for you.* Another in a long list He had yet to answer.

*   *   *

Daniel couldn't believe what had happened. *I actually forgot about my job interview.* He had been anticipating this opportunity for days, and all it took was a few damsels in distress for him to lose sight of his goals. He walked briskly until reaching the tailor's shop, and paused for a moment to glance in the store window's mirror. He straightened his narrow black tie and smoothed out the wrinkles from his best trousers. At least they were dark pants. He didn't have nearly the mud splatters the two young ladies were wearing when he left them.

Anna. What a lovely name. What a lovely girl. Her eyes had sparked flashes of fire at the unjust treatment of her friend. What color were her eyes? Green? Blue? They were beautiful, just like Anna. After her hat flew off her head even her mussed-up hair did not diminish her beauty. *Daniel, you shouldn't even be thinking such thoughts. Your plans do not include involvement with any woman.*

He set his musings aside as he hurried to his interview. He came to a two-story brick building, the home of a regional magazine publisher. He wasn't unhappy at the newspaper, but broadening his experience in journalism would be advantageous in bolstering his career. Ultimately, he *needed* job promotions to provide for his mother and sister and keep them from falling into the pit of poverty from which they had escaped. He tried three times to open the front door.

Locked.

Alarmed, he banged on the door, but all was quiet. He peered through the glass window, cupping his hands around his face to see inside. He thought he saw movement in the back of the room. He knocked again, more calmly this time. He heard the lock turn, and the door opened just enough to see the wrinkled face of an old man.

"What do you want? We're closed."

"I'm Daniel Wright. I have a job interview today. Supposed to be at eleven o'clock."

"Well, it's not eleven o'clock now, is it, sonny? Used to be eleven o'clock, but you darn well missed your time."

"I know, but if you could just tell Mr. Jackson I'm here, maybe he will see me."

"Can't do it."

"Why not?"

"Gone. You ought to thank your lucky stars. He was pacing the floor, checking his pocket watch every few minutes, glancing at the wall clock, muttering to himself. Never a good sign. If you'd gotten here while he was still here, he would've given you what for."

"Can I talk with him tomorrow? Ask for another chance?"

"If you know what's good for you, you'll forget about any job here. He's a bear to work for. Chases most everyone away. That's why there's always a job opening. He works people into the ground and then they quit."

"How long have you been here?"

"Well, can't right tell for sure. A long time."

"Why haven't you been chased away?"

The man got a twinkle in his eye, and a sad smile. "I guess when you're the man's father, and you know him better than most, you're more willing to put up with him. Guess I'm the only one who can."

Daniel nodded. "Thank you for your time."

He forced a smile, turned away, and let out a sigh to release the pent-up pressure from missing his interview. Maybe it was for the best. Ironic he would encounter two bad employers in one day. So many gave no thought to those they stepped on. He remembered the day his family lost their first home. At ten years old he had witnessed the injustice of losing their land and their livelihood. Immoral men preyed on weak men, like his father. He thought of Anna and Ruby. James Morgan's many misdeeds flooded his mind. The man had no scruples, provided it fattened his bank account.

The last hard-hitting article Daniel published had raised questions about Morgan's integrity, and stirred up a hornets' nest, but served as a warning to the man to tread more lightly. Suddenly, he knew what he would do—write another investigative piece on Morgan, and how misuse of power hurts a community.

Inspecting his pocket watch, he hurried to the home he shared with his mother and sister, the exact wording he'd use to write the article already coming together in his mind.

CHAPTER 2

Daniel removed his dress jacket in the front hallway and hung it on the coat stand. He glanced around the cheerful two-story abode his mother and sister had made into a loving home, thankful every day they were no longer living in the crowded apartment they had been forced into when they lost his childhood home. And yet, he was painfully aware how quickly they could again return to poverty.

"Well, you are home early." Daniel's sister, Susan, approached, holding a question in her eyes.

"Yes, but I need to work on a new article."

She nodded. "You're in time for tea. I baked an apple spice cake too."

"Smells good." He followed his younger sister into the sitting room, the calm of the blue floral décor a relief and the table set as if he were expected. Mother was already enjoying her small meal.

"Daniel. I hoped you would join us. How was your interview?"

He disliked being the bearer of bad news, especially after he saw his mother's expectant look. He sat down and shook his head as Susan poured him a cup of tea.

"Hmm. Not good I see." His mother sipped from her cup, eyes locked on him, waiting.

"No. This morning definitely did not go as planned."

The women listened intently as he explained what had happened. His mother leaned forward and patted his hand. "Honey, I would have been more surprised if you had not stopped to help those two poor women. I raised you well."

"I think he should have done more." Susan's words caught Daniel off guard.

"What more could I have done?"

"I think you should have spoken directly to Morgan before he had a chance to push them both into the mud."

"He didn't exactly push them, and you know our history with Morgan. My involvement any sooner would have made things worse, especially since the ladies were doing a fine job pleading their case." He took a bite of his cake. "Besides, I have my own idea about how to handle Morgan."

"What idea?" his mother asked.

"I plan to write an investigative piece about his business dealings. He deserves to have his illegal operations exposed and to pay for his crimes."

"Are you sure this is wise, son?" His mother fidgeted with her cloth napkin. "We know from personal experience what a man like Morgan can do."

He saw the uncertainty in her eyes. His responsibilities as head of their household weighed heavily on him. Carefree days were few since they lost their home and his father had abdicated life. "What else can I do? I did not get the job. I will not be bringing in more money and I need a way to advance at the paper. A hard-hitting article would help. And maybe bring down Morgan, too."

His mother poured herself more tea. "Let God handle Morgan."

"You mean the way God handled him when he booted us out of our home?"

"Oh, here we go again." Susan pushed her chair away and cleared the table, grabbed the utensils with a quiet fury, and stomped to the kitchen counter.

Their mother gasped. "Susan."

Daniel's sister dropped the spoons with a heavy clatter into the sink, and then turned to face him. "I have a better idea. I joined the women's suffrage movement. I think you should get involved, too."

"What?"

"You heard me."

He looked at his mother. "Did you know?"

"Yes. I fully support her."

"What good will involvement with suffrage do?" he asked.

"If we had the vote," his mother said, "we could push for fewer gambling places, less alcohol, maybe even prohibition. Wouldn't life have been better if those establishments weren't so accessible to your father?"

"You think this is what women's voting is about?"

"It's an example of how women could make a difference if they had a voice."

Daniel nodded. "Makes sense."

"Besides," Susan added. "Think of the trouble Mother and I had setting up our dress shop. Without your name added to the lease, I don't believe the owner would have rented to us. Meanwhile, men do business in this town every day with little more than a handshake."

Jingling his keys, a nervous habit he was trying to break, Daniel said, "I see your point."

"There's a meeting this afternoon," Susan said, her voice filled with a confidence he'd rarely seen. "The vote is coming up in two months and I have read almost nothing in your precious paper about suffrage. Report, and inform your readers."

"The story has possibilities," he said, grabbing a notepad to scribble some ideas. "The movement isn't without controversy. My editor may have stayed away from the story for good reason, but if well researched, the impact could be huge."

"What better way to support me and mother, and other women like the two you helped this morning? This can be your way to help give us a voice."

Daniel's mind raced. He could do a series of articles on the movement, but he'd also be wading into a river of unpredictable rapids. The fellows at the paper were divided on the issue of women's suffrage, and he didn't know where his boss stood.

Something this contentious could cost him his job. Then what would he do? Mother's dress shop did well for a small business, but couldn't be their sole support. And yet, if he used this movement to expose employers like Morgan, maybe there would be more choices for women. All businesses would improve. And Morgan would lose some of his power.

"Did you hear me?" Susan touched his shoulder. "I have to leave for my meeting."

"Let's go."

"You're coming to a women's meeting?"

"Yes. And no." He grinned. "I'll wait outside and interview some of the ladies afterwards. I should gather some good information from them."

He helped his mother with her light overcoat and handed her a black umbrella to keep her dry as she walked back to her dress shop for the afternoon's business. As they parted, he wondered if he would ever make enough to support them without the need for his mother to work. Yes, God provided for them, but barely. Hardships dogged them.

Was he making their lives worse by stirring up trouble with his stories? No time for such thoughts. He had his job. This time, he would make a difference.

*   *   *

Anna and Ruby arrived at Dr. Thompson's beautiful two-story Victorian home, its turrets and lovely bay windows prominent. The door was held open as several ladies streamed in ahead of them. A bright smiling face belonging to an elegantly dressed lady wearing a floor length peach empire waist gown with a matching long-sleeved floral print covering, welcomed each person.

"How do you do?" The woman, in her late thirties, exuded self-confidence. "My name is Esther Thompson. Welcome to my home."

"Thank you very much," Anna said.

She and Ruby made their way to the living area and found seats among the circle of green upholstered chairs. She noticed the furniture matched the tapestry papered walls' colors of bold burgundy, green, and cream colors, embellished by pink roses and accented by gold tones. The chandelier's cut crystals interplayed with the flames from the crackling fire creating a whimsical shimmering effect, and the kaleidoscope colors brightened the room. Women conversed among themselves, and Anna nodded to a few neighborhood women whom she recognized.

"Ladies, ladies. I call this meeting to order." Esther's voice, sweet but determined, rang through the air. "As you know, our president, Mrs. Irma Addison, has been very ill, and has tendered her resignation. I will run the meeting today, but I want you to have time to consider who should replace Irma. She was our president for many years and did a wonderful job when we were helping at the hospital or the orphanage, but we need to consider how we can win the vote for women's suffrage. We need to think a little differently about our mission and our goals."

"What?" An old woman known as Miss Betty spoke up. "Did you say we're missing our goats?"

"No, Miss Betty. I'm talking about what kind of goals we need for our club."

Anna and Ruby's eyes met. They both hid their faces to keep from laughing and Anna admired the kind way Esther spoke to the older woman.

"All right, then," Miss Betty replied, sitting straighter and thumping her cane on the wood floor. I was just gonna say, my papa had goats and they were always escaping. More trouble than they're worth. Glad we don't actually have none." Miss Betty turned to the secretary. "Can you please record that I don't think it's a good idea to ever get goats?"

The secretary nodded, smiled, and scribbled some notes on her pad of paper.

Esther's eyes danced with humor. "Now, let us hear some ideas on what we can do to help the suffrage movement in our community."

The women, most dressed in colorful finery with wide-brimmed hats decorated with ribbons or flowers and artfully set on their pompadour hairstyles, sat in silence. Anna glanced around the room. Most were staring at their black short-vamped shoes, avoiding eye contact.

"Um, we could have a bake sale," a dark-haired woman suggested tentatively.

"What would we do with the money we raise?" Esther asked.

The woman shrugged her shoulders. "We could send the funds to the state or national headquarters. I don't know. You know I like to bake."

A few snickers erupted around them.

"I think she has the right idea," Anna said, and the dark-haired woman cast her a grateful look. "We take the skills we have and use them to promote the cause, to get people to listen and educate them, and they will support women's suffrage."

"But it's the men who are going to vote yes or no on something which affects us." The older silver-haired woman narrowed her gaze toward her. "How do we win them over?"

"I think we use more than one strategy." She observed the other women in the circle. "First, we can use the idea to have a bake sale, pies, because we all know men love pie, and the way to a man's heart is through his stomach."

"Hear, hear. Some things never change," another woman added. Approving smiles, chuckles, and whispers emanated throughout the room.

"Second, we educate the women on how good this will be for their families, and those who are married will enlighten their men." Anna frowned when she saw blank faces.

"As much as my husband loved me," Ruby spoke up, "he didn't listen to me on matters he considered to be men's business. I don't think he would have listened to me about this either. He would say I didn't know enough to make these kinds of decisions."

"I see your point, but this will be more than one conversation," Anna explained. "We will need real talking. Maybe some battles. The question is whether you believe suffrage is worth fighting for.

Maybe we need to use our voice in our own homes to have a voice outside of them."

A thoughtful silence fell over the room. Then a few women clapped. Esther joined in with an approving smile which touched Anna deeply. "Bravo, Anna. Well said. Do you have any other suggestions before we break for lunch?"

"Well, yes." Anna was surprised by the number of ideas her mind was generating. "We should have a series of events to publicize the vote, and have it culminate in one big rally downtown, with speakers, prior to voting day, just like politicians do. We could have red, white, and blue banners and other decorations, signs with messages on them, and maybe a band to help draw a crowd. Perhaps a well-known suffrage leader would be willing to participate as well."

"Anna, I think I speak for all here that we are certainly blessed by your presence today." Heads nodded and words of agreement drifted over the room.

"Let's have lunch and then vote for our new president," Esther said.

As they moved to the dining area, a few women thanked Anna for her inspiring words.

"I didn't know you could speak so eloquently," Ruby exclaimed.

"What do you mean?" Anna asked as she took a few finger sandwiches from a crystal serving platter.

Ruby shook her head, a coy smile reserved for Anna alone. "You don't know, do you?"

Anna raised an eyebrow, puzzled by her friend's

words.

"Ladies, take your seats please," Esther voice was full of anticipation. "We have had a request to commence the vote for president, but first I want to bless our food and the remainder of our time together."

They bowed their heads.

"Great God in heaven, we thank thee for the plentiful bounty you have bestowed on us. Thank you for your provision and your guidance in all matters great and small. You have blessed us with strong hands to work and strong minds to think. Let us not forget they are from you. Give us wisdom as we go forward with your work in our world. In Jesus' name."

A chorus of *"amens"* sounded.

Anna couldn't help but smile at Esther's beautiful words. *I have no doubt God hears her prayers.* She'd only just met the woman, but her admiration for Esther grew.

"Now ladies, we know the months ahead will be filled with challenges, much work, and great commitment." Esther continued, bringing Anna back to the task at hand. "My prayer is for one accord with our vote. Who do you think would be a good president? We need someone with a fit mind, a good heart, and the passion and words to promote our cause."

Just then, Anna's embroidered cloth napkin fell to the floor and she reached down to retrieve it. When she straightened, she was startled to see all eyes were on her. They were pointing. *At her.*

"All in favor of electing Anna Bailey as the *new* president of our Women's Club, say aye."

Like an echo bouncing around the room, came a series of "ayes" as the women whole-heartedly gave their approval.

Esther gave a quick sweep across the room. "No need to see if there are any opposed. Congratulations, Anna." Esther's face beamed. "You are our new president."

All the smiling faces added to her confusion. "But I have never led anything. How can this be?"

"My dear, I believe God brought you to us this day. For this very purpose."

Anna shook her head in disbelief.

"Please say you will accept." Esther's eyes sparkled with approval. "I will help you. We all will. You will not be alone."

Anna saw the reassuring nods from the other women, the excitement etched on their faces.

What will my family say? I am not sure I can do this. Swallowing hard, she asked, "Are you certain? I do not want to let you down."

Esther gently touched her arm. "No, my dear. I am sure you won't."

She knew she would need more help than these ladies could give her, but what else could she do? *Daniel*. He could help them through his newspaper.

"All right then," she said, forcing a hopeful, yet uncertain smile. "I accept."

*   *   *

Daniel paced in front of the Thompson's home,

growing more nervous by the minute. As a seasoned reporter, he didn't expect to be uncomfortable waiting outside a house full of women. He also should have known a women's meeting could last for hours. He finally leaned against a tree, hoping he didn't appear suspicious.

He relaxed as he appreciated the majestic view of Elliot Bay, the surrounding forests misted in fog, and the myriad of homes and buildings which were evidence of the rapid growth of the area. He pulled his coat a little tighter against the chill of the wind.

Finally, the door opened. A few groups of two to three women left at a time and he stepped forward.

"Excuse me ladies, I'm Daniel Wright, newspaper reporter for the Seattle Post Intelligencer." He flashed his press credentials, but at first none would talk to him.

Finally, an older woman stopped. "You will want to talk to our new president. Just elected today. She'll be able to answer all your questions."

The other two women nodded and smiled. One added, "She is just the person you need to speak with."

He heard the same thing repeatedly, as if read from a script. Even his sister echoed a similar sentiment, except she also said, "Our new president is wonderful. You will really like her."

Curious, he stayed, and waited some more. His stomach gurgled. He knew he should have eaten more than the sweet cake his sister had made in the early morning, but there was little else in the house.

The door opened again. Two young women

emerged and stood on the covered porch supported by white pillars and adorned with lavender wisteria. They stared at him. *Could it be? Yes, Anna and Ruby.* Another woman, presumably the doctor's wife, said her good-byes and closed the door.

Compelled, he watched Anna, the lovely girl who made his thoughts turn incoherent, and his words turn to mush. *How can I interview her, especially when what I really want is to court her?*

*　　*　　*

Anna stepped off the Thompson's covered porch with Ruby by her side and stopped to admire the abundance of flowers and the sweet lingering fragrance.

"Is that Daniel?" Ruby asked.

Anna peered out across the lawn. "Yes, I believe it is." Her breath caught for a moment, and her heart beat in double time. Memories of the sparkle in his eyes when he last talked to her flooded her senses as she walked straight toward him. "I'm going to ask him to write an article for his newspaper."

"Good afternoon, Anna, Ruby," Daniel greeted. "You attended the meeting?"

"Yes." Thrilled to see him again so soon, Anna fiddled with her handbag to keep from staring.

"What are you doing here?" Ruby asked.

"Waiting to interview the new president of the women's club."

"You're looking at her," Ruby said with pride in her voice.

"You?" Daniel stepped toward Ruby.

"Oh no, not me. It's Anna."

Daniel stepped back again and Anna's cheeks warmed as his gaze shifted back to her. "They must have seen your leadership qualities, Miss Bailey."

"Thank you, Mr. Wright." She pressed her hand onto her head to keep her hair from being blown into her face by the wind. She laughed at her own awkwardness.

He flashed her a quick grin.

His gaze almost made her forget what she'd planned to say. "I wanted to talk to you about helping us." *Why can't I look him in the eye now?* Her cheeks grew even warmer, and she forgot her words, her thoughts. She forgot everything. When she glanced again, he was staring at her, as if he could see into her soul.

"How can I be of service?"

Was he possibly even more attractive than she'd remembered from this morning? She liked the way a stray dark curl had escaped his smoothed hair and was hanging over his forehead, free to roam with the unpredictable passing breezes.

"Anna?" Ruby shook her shoulder.

"I'm sorry. I was just thinking. Where were we?"

Daniel wore a sweet grin on his face. "I wanted to know how I can help you, but I think we should set up a time to meet. Can I take you to dinner? I would like to interview you for an article I'm writing on the local suffrage movement. We can also discuss what I can do to help you."

Anna gave a nervous laugh. "I wanted to talk to you about the very same thing."

But this almost sounds like a date and I have not cared for anyone since high school when Benjamin betrayed me. She wasn't ready for emotional attachments with any man. Was she?

"Perfect," Ruby said. "Daniel, why don't you call on her at six o'clock tonight and find a quiet restaurant where you two can talk."

"We don't have to be formal." Anna said, quelling the panic rising within her.

"Don't be silly." Ruby glanced deviously at Daniel. "Are you available for dinner and an interview tonight?"

Daniel hesitated. Was he uncomfortable too?

"Yes, this suits me. Anna?"

She nodded, even as myriad reasons to say no crowded her mind. "Yes, I can come."

It's all right. This is only an interview.

"I have to work at the office until six. Could I meet you at six-thirty at Giuseppe's Italian Restaurant, and then escort you home after?"

She gave him a tentative smile, wishing to be amiable, while red flags signaled to her to run away. Daniel represented danger. She swallowed hard and her chest tightened. "Yes, that will be fine."

"I look forward to it," Daniel added in a warm, husky voice.

After Anna walked away, she glanced back and saw that he still stood there, watching. She took deep breaths to calm down.

"Oh, how wonderful." Ruby gushed.

As the cold wind blew stronger, Anna raised the collar on her coat to stop her shivering. "What are you talking about?"

"You and Daniel. You will spend time together and get to know each other. You never know where it might lead."

"The interview will lead to a news story which will help with passing the right to vote for women." She walked faster. "That's where it will lead. Nothing more."

"I wouldn't be so close-minded."

Anna stopped. "We have a job, a mission, one I think God has called me to do. I am not going to let myself be distracted by a man, just because he's attractive."

"Ah ha—you do think he's handsome, then?"

Anna started walking again. "I never said he wasn't."

"But he's also really nice. He could be the one for you."

"He seems nice, but things are not always as they seem."

"Are you referring to what happened with your teacher, and with Benjamin?" When Anna didn't respond, Ruby continued, "That's it, isn't it?"

Anna's throat tightened as memories of Benjamin flooded her senses. How could the hurt remain after so long? With deep wounds carved on her heart, how would she ever be able to view another man without doubts or suspicion? "Please, let's talk of something else."

They reached the front of Ruby's boarding house and Ruby turned to face her. "I wish you'd give him a chance."

"I have to go," Anna said, avoiding her.

"Anna, it's been five years! Not every man is

like Benjamin. Or like Mr. Hargrove either."

"That remains to be seen."

Anna hurried away, not wanting to think of the hurt still festering due to a devastating episode in high school, when she discovered her college entrance exams torn up in her teacher's wastebasket. Mr. Hargrove had never submitted them for college scholarships on her behalf because she was a female. And Benjamin, her first love, had known, and didn't care.

CHAPTER 3

Anna arrived home excited to tell her father and sister, Nellie, about her new role in the women's suffrage group, hoping to win their support. However, when she opened the door her sister's eyes widened as she gasped at Anna's appearance.

"Anna, what happened to you?" Nellie's face showed concern as she grasped Anna's mud-splattered skirt, holding a section out and examining the fabric. "Are you all right?"

"Yes, I am fine. I'll change clothes and then I will explain."

Nellie frowned, but nodded her assent.

An hour later, Nellie and her father sat at their dark mahogany dining room table as Anna explained the events of her day and the new role she'd accepted. They were attentive, but too quiet.

"Well?" Anna asked. "What do you think?"

Nellie gave Anna a reassuring hug as she rose from the ornately carved high-backed chair. "Well, you were put in a difficult position." She dished up more soup for her father from the large pot on the wood stove and placed the earthen bowl in front of him. "I can understand why they would want such a clever young woman as you, but are you sure this is what *you* want?"

The intensity of Nellie's gaze made Anna uncomfortable. "Yes, I am certain. I believe, based on what happened today, I am supposed to do this."

Nellie fussed with the dishes, avoided eye contact, and said, "All right then."

Their gray-haired father pushed his wire rim glasses back over the bridge of his nose, his stoic face not revealing what he thought of Anna's new venture. This response wasn't new. As a seminary professor he pondered things. Considered them deeply before he ever spoke. He was part philosopher, theologian, and father, all rolled into one, and this was what made him an excellent teacher.

"Anna, if you lead suffrage with the same conviction you demonstrate in other areas, I know you will do well." He stood, rested his hands on her shoulders, and placed a gentle kiss on her forehead.

"Thank you, Father."

He smiled. "Time to head to my study. I need to grade papers for tomorrow."

Anna watched as her father ambled down the hall. Her heart swelled with love for the man she'd come to see as her rock, the one dependable force in her world, especially since her mother had died six years ago, on Anna's sixteenth birthday.

Nellie shook her head. "Are you sure you should go to dinner tonight with a man you just met?"

Anna finished her small glass of milk and stood to help with the dishes. "This is only a dinner interview, and nothing more."

"I want you to be safe, and to keep your good reputation." Nellie placed a firm hand on Anna's arm and spun her around, searching her eyes. "You are my younger sister, *and* my best friend."

Anna smiled, unsure why Nellie was acting like this. "What are your concerns?" she asked as she turned away and filled the sink with water.

Handing Anna the small stack of soup bowls, Nellie's mouth drew tight as she said, "I wouldn't want gossip to ruin your chances for a match with a man of good reputation. I'd like you to find someone like Samuel."

"Your beau suits you well, but I need someone a little less serious. Someone who is full of laughter, as well as dependable. I don't even know if there is such a man. Maybe I will stay as I am and take care of father."

Nellie's eyes widened. "You don't mean it."

Anna stiffened, unsettled by her sister's incredulous tone. "I don't have anything else to say."

"All right." Nellie rattled the pans as she put them away in the cupboard. "Your support for suffrage could cost father his job. There are many opposed who would go to great lengths to keep suffrage from passing. Your tutoring jobs could suffer. And our housekeeper quit today."

"Well that's unfortunate. However, I don't see what the lack of a housekeeper has to do with suffrage. You have such a worry bug about you."

Anna scrunched up her face and made pouty lips, which always made her sister laugh.

Nellie regarded her for a moment, then giggled. "Yes. I do have the worry bug, just like mother."

Anna wrapped her arms around Nellie, held tight, and peered into her sister's face. "You remind me of her, with your red ringlets and blue eyes; but also, you have her nature."

Nellie's eyes softened, moistened for a moment. "Thank you."

"It is true, but maybe I'm trying to soften you a bit. I hoped you would help me with the suffrage events."

Nellie's brows shot up. The light in her eyes dimmed and she glanced away. "I think I'll be too busy with the housework and cooking with our housekeeper gone."

"All right." Confused, Anna didn't know what else to say. Her face grew warm with the awkwardness between them. She had assumed her sister would be involved because they had always worked together for church events and community gatherings in the past. Fortunately, she would have the help of Daniel, Ruby, and the other women from their fledgling women's group. For now she had to set her wonderings about Nellie aside and meet Daniel for her interview.

*   *   *

Giuseppe's, the small Italian restaurant Daniel chose for their meeting, had a quiet dignity reflected by its simple, but tasteful décor. White lace curtains, small round tables meant for two, and single white candles provided an ambiance improved on only by the sweet music of the violin which accompanied their meals. He hoped Anna wouldn't think it too extravagant or romantic for an interview. The owner, Giuseppe Amato, brought Italy to life in his humble café, and Daniel had eaten here by himself a few times, finding solace in its old-world charm.

Daniel's thoughts were stunned into silence by Anna's beauty as she entered the restaurant. Hesitating in the doorway as she searched the room for him, her emerald green and gold ankle length skirt with matching blouse and jacket shimmered, giving her the air of a princess, especially since she had her hair piled on her head in curls, covered by only a small black satin hat with its brim turned up on the side. This allowed him to view the unfettered, strawberry blonde ringlets flowing down each side of her face, leading his gaze to her long delicate neck.

He hurried over to greet her. "Anna."

"Hello." She smiled and walked toward him.

"Here." His knees wobbled as he led her to the table he'd reserved by the window overlooking a small garden, and he pulled out the red cushioned chair for her. The seat's legs stuck for a moment as he scooted her closer to their table, decorated with a red and white checkered cloth. The white candle in the center flickered as the chair bumped the side of the wood. "I'm sorry."

"I'm fine."

He grinned. *Yes. Finer than fine.* "Do you mind if I ask questions while we eat dinner?"

"Not at all."

Daniel drew out his notepad and pencil, conscious of the way she held her head high as her dancing eyes surveyed him and their surroundings. He swallowed hard, but his mouth was as dry as cotton and he doubted he'd be able to say two coherent words, let alone eat, with such a beautiful entrancing woman by his side. But he would try. He cleared his throat. And tried not to stare.

She leaned forward. "What kind of questions would you like to ask?"

Was she interested in him? Anna's face was like that of an angel; with soft pale skin, a smattering of freckles which spoke of her Irish heritage, high cheekbones, and blue-green eyes ordained to flash fire one moment and send their gentle approval to you in another. Yes, the face of an angel.

"Do you have questions for me?" she asked again, her expression puzzled.

Her eagerness gave him the courage he needed. "So, tell me, how long have you been involved with women's rights, with the right to vote?"

She glanced at a clock on the wall. "Almost seven hours now."

Her quick-witted response relaxed him, and they both laughed.

Daniel shook his head. "You mean you haven't had any involvement before today?"

"No, absolutely none. I should say this is the first action I've taken. I am well read. I stay up on current events, and I've done research at the library and used my father's extensive home library."

"Where did you go to college?"

"I never went." Sorrow passed over her face briefly, then was gone. "I did, however, enjoy the mentorship of my father, who is a professor at the seminary." The light in her eyes brightened once again. "I'm also pursuing publication with a magazine."

"I'm glad to hear this. Someone as intelligent as you deserves to go as far as they possibly can."

Anna sat back and Daniel's pulse quickened when he noticed how she studied him.

"I am afraid there are few men who believe women should use their minds," she continued. "In fact, some would even say God must have made a mistake in giving a woman a good mind since they should only work in the home. I am sure some of the opposition to women voting is tied to the same kind of thinking."

Daniel managed to write some notes on his pad, despite his trembling fingers, but for the most part, his thoughts wandered. *If only we were meeting sometime in the future, when my life was more settled, when my career prospects were secure, when I knew I could provide for those I love. Love? No. This is business only.*

Time passed quickly as they ate their meal and talked. The moonlight slipping through their window added a soft glow to Anna's skin and a shimmer to her curls. Mesmerized, he couldn't help but watch her. Violin music in the background set his mind on her, not the interview.

She averted her eyes.

He hadn't meant to make her uncomfortable. The truth was, he couldn't help himself. She had proved to be more captivating than he had imagined.

"Miss Bailey, Anna, you must always believe God made you strong for a reason. A good mind is something to be thankful for, and to use."

"Thank you, Daniel."

Her eyes welled up with tears of gratitude.

He believed in encouraging others, knowing the difference for him when his mother had done so. He was about to ask more about her background when he saw Anna stiffen as she stared at the front of the restaurant. He followed her gaze.

James Morgan handed his overcoat and top hat to the hostess and waited to be seated. They both watched as a waitress led him right by their table.

"Well, well," Morgan greeted, a hard edge to his words. "What do we have here? I wondered if you two were conspiring together. I was right." James Morgan's cheeks reddened, betraying the smile pasted on his face.

"Mr. Morgan, please, consider giving Ruby her job back. She is kind, honest, and hard working. She did not deserve the harshness of your judgment," Anna said defensively.

The cold smile vanished, and his voice raised a notch. "Young lady, I have the power to hire and fire, and to make sure Ruby doesn't work anywhere again. I do not care if you approve of my decisions."

"Why would you make decisions which hurt others?" she persisted.

"Well, someone has to."

Morgan roared with laughter.

Daniel quelled his anger by taking a few deep breaths. He remembered at age ten, the man's smirk as he stood on their front porch and showed his father legal papers proving *he* was the new owner of *their* farm. The eviction notice was effective immediately. Daniel had watched his father become a broken man. Even now, Morgan's business dealings were questionable at best, and his corruption was whispered about in many back rooms. But how to find proof? And not jeopardize his job or future.

The waitress stepped forward. "Mr. Morgan, I'm receiving complaints from other customers. You're disturbing their meals."

Morgan glared at Anna. His eyes narrowed and he lowered his voice, saying gruffly, "See what you did? I don't need negative attention when I'm running for office."

Daniel rose, motioned to Anna, and pulled out her chair to show he and Anna were leaving.

"Yes, take her back home where she belongs," Morgan taunted.

"Shall we go?" Anna turned from Morgan as if to dismiss him. "Good evening."

Daniel took her arm and they walked away, stopping only a moment to tell the waitress to put their meal on his newspaper's account.

Clearly, there would be no peace until Morgan

was exposed.

CHAPTER 4

Daniel stayed awake half the night working on his piece for the paper, but lack of sleep hadn't dampened his energy level or clarity concerning his proposal. He hoped his editor, Mr. Shaw, would be in a good mood, recognize a great story, and even embrace the rightness of the suffrage movement.

Daniel passed a row of identical old wooden desks, nodded to coworkers who glanced up from their work. "Hey Henry, how's it going?"

His co-worker grunted and rolled his eyes. "Deadlines, as usual."

Daniel nodded, set his briefcase down, and took out the article to present to his boss. He knocked on Shaw's office door and waited.

"Come in."

The brusque tone set Daniel on edge.

Piles of paper scattered across the desk clued Daniel for the need to be brief. "Good morning, Mr.

Shaw."

"Yes, what is it? You can see I'm up to my eyebrows in projects." He leaned back in his brown padded chair, fingering his pen, and glanced at the folder Daniel held. "What've you got there?"

"Sir, I've come across a story which deserves to be told, to be given more importance than it's received up until now. The suffrage movement from a local perspective."

Shaw leaned forward with an outstretched arm. He took the folder, laid the proposed article open on top of his other work, and appeared to scan the piece.

Daniel couldn't tell if Shaw was scowling or deep in thought. He made some notes in the side margins, then crossed out a large portion of the piece in the middle and handed it back in silence.

"Daniel, you're a good reporter. A good writer too."

"Thank you, sir."

"But there's a fine line between reporting a story and implicating individuals in activities for which you have no proof. Unless you want to put us out of business, don't name any one individual, especially James Morgan."

"But sir—"

"Let me finish." His boss rose and paced the floor, hands clasped behind his back, and head down. "I have stayed away from the suffrage movement stories. Didn't want to add to the divisiveness of the issue. But the vote is in less than two months and our readers deserve to know both sides of the story."

He stopped pacing and studied Daniel. "This is what I'll do. I want you to rewrite this piece without mentioning Morgan, add action through events the suffragettes are holding, and we will see how it's received. If there's enough substance for a series as you propose, then we will move forward with publication."

Daniel nodded. "Thank you, but surely you see men like Morgan are part of the problem."

"Whether I do or not is immaterial right now. You cannot go on a personal crusade against men like Morgan without serious repercussions."

"Yes, sir."

Shaw headed to the door to open it. "Just remember, Daniel," he said, pausing for a moment, "a good newspaperman will keep his personal bias in check. I want you to continue to do well in your career."

Daniel backed out of the room fingering his folder. "Yes, sir. Thank you, sir."

Disappointed, but not surprised at the need to change direction for his article, he pulled out his note pad and jotted down some ideas. He would write the suffrage movement stories which were growing more important to him by the day, thanks to Anna. The human-interest angle and personal perspective would help him capture readers' imagination and create support on their behalf, but how would he stay neutral in his reporting?

He would never jeopardize his career by doing anything foolish. He'd worked long and hard to get where he was, but surely, if he reported honorably, he could avoid any problems. And, if he did discover something incriminating against Morgan during his investigation, there would be a way to expose him.

Morgan must be stopped. If he won his bid for city council, his influence over the town would grow. Daniel would trust God to lead him to the information he needed or find another way to remove Morgan from their city. Whispers, rumors, and innuendos all spoke of how Morgan's corruptness extended long beyond the day he cost Daniel's father their livelihood.

Daniel's investigative skills would come in handy when he covered the suffrage event at the fair. Meanwhile, he'd keep his relationship with Anna strictly business, even if she was the loveliest girl he'd ever met. He could not risk his emotions while building his career and caring for his mother and sister. His responsibilities for them were his first concern.

A little heart flutter reminded him this would not be an easy task.

*　　*　　*

Red, white, and blue banners abounded at the county fairgrounds, small American flags were handed out like penny candy, and a band played upbeat patriotic songs, while smells of freshly baked bread, roasted pork, and fried apple fritters permeated their senses. Anticipation filled the air as Anna helped the women unload their fresh homemade pies for their booth, located across from local candidates running for office.

Excitement swirled around them this sunny fall day and Anna hummed as she worked. She would make this the best event ever. Several of the women, including Ruby, had spent all the previous day baking pies in Esther Thompson's spacious modern kitchen. Her shiny new gas oven could hold four pies at a time and Anna had set up workspaces similar to a factory, assigning each woman a job equal to her skills. She was pleased Ruby excelled in making light fluffy pie crusts. If only Nellie had agreed to help, they would have had two experienced pie crust makers.

She pushed thoughts of Nellie away for now and smiled as she placed the blackberry, peach, and apple pies on display, ready to sell. On the counter, Ruby set down a box of cookbooks, *Washington Women's Cookbook: Votes for Women, Good Things to Eat*, published by Emma Smith DeVoe, the regional suffrage movement leader who now lived in Tacoma. Esther had received the books just yesterday, and Anna had barely been able to skim through them, but she was impressed. She grinned when she read, *Give us the vote and we will cook/The better for a wide outlook.* What an ingenious fundraiser. By giving women a voice, they would be fully engaged in their homes and communities and be motivated to do well in all their endeavors, including their home life.

Anna turned her attention to Ruby. "I could hardly wait to see you today."

"Why?" Ruby asked as she placed the cookbooks in two straight stacks and stored the rest under the table. Her three-year-old daughter, Emily, stood close by, a small replica of her mother, including a matching navy-blue skirt.

"Because." Anna beamed a broad smile at them both.

"Nellie said yes?"

Anna nodded and Ruby clasped her arm as tears welled up.

"She wants you to work for us on a trial basis. Since you and Emily will share an upstairs bedroom, she wonders if Emily might be too noisy for father to work in his study. I assured her that Emily is a quiet, well-behaved child." She winked at the shy blonde-haired girl, who peeked out from behind her mother's skirt.

"I—I don't know how to thank you," Ruby said, as she appeared to study the wood shavings on the ground. "I've nearly run out of money. I think I haven't been hired elsewhere because of Mr. Morgan. When I give my name, they're no longer interested in hiring me."

"Oh Ruby. Why didn't you tell me?"

"I didn't want to trouble you, Anna. But now. You've helped me again." Ruby pulled her into a hug and said, "I'll show my gratitude by being the best housekeeper and cook you've ever had."

"What's all this frivolity?" Daniel asked with a friendly smile as he leaned on the counter.

Anna smiled back, as an unaccustomed shyness washed over her. She glanced at her friend, whose bright eyes sparkled with happiness. "Ruby has agreed to be our housekeeper."

"A sound idea." Approval directed at Anna resonated from Daniel's husky voice.

"Yes. I believe so." Anna glanced down the path. A crowd of people walked their way, a sign the fair gates had opened. "Ladies, here they come."

The women checked to ensure their golden Votes for Women pins were secured on their blouses, pressed their aprons down, and took information flyers to distribute.

"Let's sell our pies." Anna's voice rang loud and true. "More importantly, let's win some hearts."

Anna moved to the front of the booth, her pulse quickening when she realized Daniel was beside her. She cleared her throat to stay focused. "Remember, ladies, have patience with those who ask honest questions or raise concerns. If you don't have an answer please direct them to me, and don't allow yourself to be pulled into disagreements."

Lord, bless the work of our hands. Direct our thoughts, words, and actions this day. Amen.

The morning passed quickly with brisk pie sales and intense conversations. Startled at the outspokenness of women opposed to the right to vote, she wondered if the men were too polite to argue with a woman. Whatever they believed, they were buying many fine home-baked pies. Several women were curious enough about the cookbook to purchase one, even at a dollar a piece. Anna's hope grew as she thought of the reasoned ideas sprinkled throughout its pages and how they would speak to women who read the book.

*   *   *

Daniel was covering the fall event for his news

article, interviewing fairgoers for their perspective, and observing the interactions at the suffrage booth. He could not help but watch Anna when he wasn't busy with a fairgoer. He hardly knew her, but she seemed like everything he would want in a wife, if he were to marry. Her passion, commitment, and loyalty were obvious, but he also saw a kindness and a loving desire to help others, even at a cost to herself.

He finished speaking with a man, glanced down the path and spotted trouble they could do without. He rushed over to Anna.

"What is the matter?" Anna asked.

"Look." Daniel nodded toward the north.

Anna gasped. A large empty booth had been transformed into an anti-suffrage display, with slogans like '*A Woman's Place is in the Home*,' and there, handing out campaign buttons and free cigars, was James Morgan, his signature top hat giving him the height he lacked.

Daniel saw how well organized they seemed to be, and the number of women working with Morgan, of all people. They were passing out balloons, pencils, and candy for the children, anything to attract people to promote their messages— anti-suffrage and James Morgan for City Council.

Like a predator on alert, Morgan caught them staring through the crowd, smirked, and tipped his hat in their direction. Then, he walked over.

"Oh no." Anna's face paled, but Daniel held her arm. They stood their ground and waited as Morgan approached. "Good afternoon, Mr. Morgan."

"What do *you* want?" Daniel's tone was barely civil, and he struggled to hold his contempt in check.

"No need to be antagonistic. I just thought I should visit the opposition." He observed the pies and the ladies, and Daniel wondered if he was taking mental notes on who was there. Fortunately, Ruby was occupied along the path, sharing with a couple with two young children.

"Would you like to buy a pie?" Anna asked. "We've been told they are quite delicious."

Anna's polite conversation was more than what Daniel could muster. *I wonder what it costs her to maintain her civility.*

"I'm sure they are, Miss Bailey, but I will not be supporting your movement even for want of a pie." Morgan raised an eyebrow as he took the foul-smelling cigar he had held behind his back, placed the stogie in his mouth, and exhaled a big puff. The putrid smoke emanating from this human chimney permeated the air around the booth and caused would-be customers to scatter. "Good day, miss."

Morgan chuckled and nodded toward Daniel and the other ladies as they coughed uncontrollably. They gagged, choked, and fanned themselves to clear the air. Morgan whistled as he turned and left, the strong odor of smoke trailing behind him.

Anna grabbed a flyer and fanned the air violently. "What a dirty trick!"

"He is a sly fox," Daniel said.

Anna's expression showed alarm. "You don't admire him, do you?"

"No. Not the way you might think."

"What then?"

"His mind. He is always thinking of his next move. He has cheated farmers out of their profits, manipulated events to gain land he never worked for, and used others' hard-earned money to build his empire."

He shook his head while past memories flooded his brain. So much effort, work, used in a wrong way. He only wished he had the same kind of business sense. "Too bad he doesn't use his shrewd business smarts for good."

"Well, we cannot dwell on Morgan, other than to be on guard against what he may do next." Anna returned to the counter, placing more pies on its surface. "We have a campaign to win."

Daniel moved next to her, warmth like an electric current waving through him at their close proximity as he handed her a pie. "Yes. Yes, *we* do."

*　　*　　*

Within thirty minutes the booth had returned to normal, and the crowds were even bigger than before. They were low on pies when Esther and Susan, Daniel's sister, showed up.

"Does anyone need pies?" Susan asked.

"How did you know?" Anna was ready to burst with thankfulness.

"Mother and I were talking after Daniel left this morning. We decided with such a beautiful day there would be quite a large turnout just clamoring for some freshly made pie, so I contacted Esther and we all got to work."

Susan's triumphant tone made Daniel laugh. "That's my sister."

A commotion at the counter drew Anna's attention away from their conversation.

"I want my money back. Worst pie ever. What are you trying to do? Salt us to death?"

Anna, Susan, and Esther moved to the front of the booth and Daniel followed. A curmudgeonly old man with gnarled hands stood with a half-eaten pie, his white mustache and unkempt long beard stained by the blackberries he'd consumed.

"I'm sorry, sir. What seems to be the problem?" Anna hoped her conciliatory voice would calm him down.

"I'm telling you. Something's wrong with this pie. Too much salt."

"How did you eat so much, then?"

"I shared part with my dog, just to be sure it weren't my taste buds. Eats anything, but even he wouldn't finish what I give 'im." A rotund spotted hound stood beside his master, wagging his tail slowly. "See, I'll show you."

He dropped a small bite to the ground. The dog sniffed. And whined. But wouldn't eat it.

"We will certainly refund your money, sir. I cannot imagine what happened. We have had no other complaints."

"Thank ye, miss."

After he was reimbursed, two more people came, claiming their pies were over-salted. One short, stocky man with day old face stubble and wearing a black derby hat looked familiar, and

Anna remembered seeing him speak to Mr. Morgan earlier.

"I demand my money back. I want satisfaction," he stormed.

"Sir, we're sorry for your inconvenience. We will certainly refund your money," Anna told him, but she suspected foul play. Glancing around, she noticed darkened eyes, furrowed brows, and worry lines etched on the other suffragette ladies' faces.

"Well, you better, or I'll be reporting you to the fair board. I have a mind to do so anyway."

"Nothing was done intentionally by our women," Anna said, her stomach twisting in knots. "They are wonderful cooks and everyone has raved about their delicious pies."

"Well, somethin' happened to make you fail this time. Maybe your pies are like this whole suffrage movement." His voice bellowed so those close by could hear. "Beautiful and tempting on the outside, but full of deceit on the inside."

Anna was shocked into silence by his statement.

Daniel came closer. "I think you're overreacting, sir. These women mean no harm to anyone. Someone is obviously trying to undermine their good work. Please take your money and leave."

The man snickered and left, money in hand.

Ruby hurried over, clearly upset. "That man. He works for Morgan. I think his name is Jed."

Anna scowled as her hope deflated under the burden of injustice which weighed heavy on her shoulders. "I should not be surprised, but Morgan sure uses dirty tricks to get his way."

Ruby nodded in agreement. "Jed would come into the hotel when I worked there and meet with Mr. Morgan at a back table in the restaurant. They weren't friends. Mr. Morgan seemed to be giving him his next job assignment."

Daniel had been listening and nodded. "Sometimes unethical businessmen will hire others to do their dirty work for them. He probably pays him on the side for special jobs. This gives me a lead, Ruby. Good work."

"We have more trouble heading our way." Anna braced for the four angry customers approaching with their pies. After they left with their refunds, sales fell to almost none.

While Daniel and Ruby looked on, Anna took out two pies to taste: one within easy reach of customers, and one set aside under the counter for a suffrage lady. She cut a slim slice of the peach pie which had been protected under the counter. *Delicious*. The second was the blackberry pie within easy reach of customers. She took a small bite.

"Ugh. Too much salt."

Daniel handed her a cup of water, and she took a big gulp.

Ruby moved in closer to examine the pie as Anna coughed and choked.

"Look," Anna wiped her mouth with a towel and pointed to the middle of the pie with an accusatory finger. "This one had sugar sprinkles baked into the crust, but if you examine the top you can tell someone also added salt after it was baked."

Ruby moved closer to inspect the pie and shook her head in disbelief. "Well, I'll be. Yes, I see."

Picking up the tainted pie, Anna dumped it with a loud thud into the trash and ceremoniously wiped her hands together. "I know we cannot prove anything, but I think Morgan's man sabotaged our pies while we were busy with other customers. I cannot believe he would stoop so low."

"Yes, Morgan would stoop low. And lower." Daniel's jaw tightened and his eyes darkened. "Ladies. I am going to scout out the situation. Maybe I can find out something useful."

Anna sighed as he left, then directed her attention toward Esther who had worked in silence during the conversation. "We can still pass out flyers, talk to people, and help them understand what is at stake with suffrage."

"Yes, or we can regroup and fight another day." Threads of compassion were interwoven throughout her tone. "I know you're disappointed, but this is not your fault dear. We need to learn and move on. We did raise some money through the cookbook sales, and we can do the same at future events."

Just then loud chants met Anna's ears along with a reverberating drumbeat, as a parade crowd walked the path toward them. "Hey hey, ho ho, the suffrage movements got to go! Hey hey, ho ho, the suffrage movements got to go!"

Four women, clothed in long black skirts and white lace blouses covered by kitchen aprons, were holding a banner which said, '*Don't destroy our families!*' Others raised rolling pins high as if they were flags. Leading the group to the right of the banner was Mr. Morgan holding a sign which read, '*James Morgan for City Council.*'

Anna met Esther's eyes. "I think you're right. We need to plan more events. We will hold rallies and have speeches to explain our position." Anna noticed one friendly person standing at their counter. "Reverend Sparks. How nice to see you."

The Reverend grinned. "Am I too late for some dessert? I visited parishioners most of the day."

Anna explained what had happened with their pies.

"I'll be happy to test them for you, and pay for my pie," Reverend Sparks said.

Moments later, Daniel returned from his search for information. "I think I'll have quite the story after today."

He eyed the Reverend enjoying the last of a slice of peach pie. "No problems, Reverend?"

"None, except I don't have room for any more."

Anna laughed. "Thank you, Reverend Sparks. I appreciate your support."

"If there's any other way I can be of service, let me know. I think you're doing important work."

She searched his face and saw sincerity, conviction, and respect. "I—I do have an idea. A thought just came to me."

He and Daniel both looked at her with curiosity, while the others cleaned the booth. "I'm wondering if I might have permission to speak during tomorrow morning's church service, to share the importance of the suffrage movement."

Hesitant, she held her breath until she saw a small grin grow into a large smile on the Reverend's face. "An excellent idea."

He paused, deep in thought. "First, I will share

some of your experiences here today, and tell them about your delicious pie. Then I'll turn the pulpit over to you."

The Reverend rose and gave them both a slight bow. "Until tomorrow."

"Thank you, Reverend," she replied, and watched as the tall lanky man in the dark sack coat nodded and left with a bounce in his step.

Anna's heart raced as she sat in silence with Daniel beside her, then asked, "What have I done? I've never spoken to a crowd before."

Her throat constricted as she imagined standing in front of the sanctuary with parishioners filling the pews, all eyes on her as she spoke.

Daniel leaned toward her and she noted the soft kindness in his eyes. With quiet confidence he gently said, "Anna, you spoke with conviction to Reverend Sparks just now. Once you begin speaking, you will share those same persuasive thoughts for all to hear."

Anna certainly hoped so.

CHAPTER 5

Daniel, Susan, and his mother had taken seats close to the front of the simple, rough-hewn church. He made sure to sit with a clear view of Anna when she rose to speak. He had not realized the large size of this wood-framed structure, nor how many parishioners called First Free Methodist Church their home. The high-backed dark pews were purposely uncomfortable, designed to keep members awake, but so far he had found the service spiritually uplifting, unlike the ornate church he and his family regularly attended. He noticed a number of people he knew, including Ruby and her daughter sitting to his left and Dr. and Mrs. Thompson beside Anna's family.

During the singing of a hymn, Daniel chuckled as he recalled Susan's whispered words.

I packed a picnic lunch for you and Anna in case you would like to interview her again. Her knowing smile told him she had turned matchmaker. He had never been so excited about a possible picnic before and had to tamp down his enthusiasm, in order to stay focused on the present.

Reverend Sparks cut his sermon short and gave an introduction for Anna. He expounded on her character, her service to the church and community, and her passion to share why the suffrage movement was important for everyone. Several people leaned over whispering to their companions creating a low rumble.

Reverend Sparks cleared his throat. "I expect you to listen to our dear sister's words with an open mind and let the spirit of God lead you this day into all His truth. Anna?"

Daniel had glanced at Anna throughout the service. She had been reading her notes and finding scriptures in her Bible. Her father patted Anna's hand as she rose.

Daniel observed a red-haired woman on her father's other side, wearing a light-blue satin hat adorned with small white flowers. The woman's unnatural posture drew his attention, sitting ramrod straight as if she would never bend, only break. Her sullen countenance reflected the sour face of her companion, a man no older than she. *Why does she look familiar?*

With a halting step Anna walked forward and climbed the stairs to the podium. She had worn a plain black skirt this morning and a high-necked white blouse adorned with simple lace. Her hair was pulled back in the pompadour style, and partly hidden under the same small black velvet hat she'd worn during their dinner. She probably had not wanted to draw attention to herself, but Daniel realized she would be lovely no matter what she wore.

Daniel sat up straighter, writing pad in hand, ready to scribble down notes from what Anna would share. He had a lump in his throat watching her and wished he could carry her burden.

"I am here today to speak about the suffrage movement and to explain a reasoned Biblical basis for women to vote. There has been much misinformation given by those opposed, in order to scare people into restricting voting for men alone. Because women love their husbands and their children, they will vote for ideas and individuals with the goal of strengthening families, not destroying them.

"Some say women do not know enough about subjects to vote on them, but if women can search the scriptures to find truth for daily living, they can also take a subject from a ballot and research those issues as well.

"We find examples of women in the Bible who God used to speak to their times. In the Old Testament, Queen Esther spoke at the right time and saved her people from destruction at the hands of Haman. Deborah, the judge, was a bold woman known not just for her wisdom but for her courage. In the New Testament, a Jewish woman named Priscilla, along her husband, bravely shared the gospel. Even as a wife, Priscilla was outspoken about what mattered.

"God gave women a voice during Biblical times to work out His purposes. Would He not still give women a voice today, as a way to work His good will in our families, our community, our nation, and our world? Please, prayerfully consider this issue and vote as the Lord directs. Thank you."

Anna smiled as the sound of thunderous applause bounced off the walls and echoed throughout the sanctuary. Daniel had never seen parishioners clap in church before, but Anna's words had struck a chord and he prayed the message would be remembered. Mesmerized while she spoke, he realized he'd not taken a single note. He was in awe of this lovely lady, her eloquence, passion, and commitment coming through not just in her speech, but in the way she lived her life. He could easily love her.

Maybe I do love her. He hoped more time together during their picnic lunch would shed some light on his feelings.

And hers.

*   *   *

While she spoke, Anna knew her words resonated with many. She watched their faces soften, their body language change from crossed arms to leaning forward in their seats, and nods of agreement from the ladies and the gentlemen. All but a few. Unfortunately, Nellie and her beau, Samuel, were among those who remained unmoved, a scowl pasted on their faces as if they had just swallowed cod liver oil. After Anna finished, her knees wobbled as she descended the stairs and joined the crowd which had come forward to talk with her. Some had questions, others encouraged her, and several shared how her talk had deeply touched them.

As the crowd dispersed, she caught sight of Daniel coming from one direction and her family from another.

Her father touched her arm. "Dear, what a most convincing talk on women having a voice in our society. I am truly impressed and grateful to God for using you as His instrument."

His face radiated joy and the light in his eyes reflected his approval, a gift she readily embraced.

God, maybe you hear me more than I think you do.

Nellie and Samuel stood nearby, obviously uncomfortable, and Anna couldn't understand why. She'd have a sincere talk with her sister soon.

But for the moment, she couldn't help but smile when Daniel approached with a huge grin on his face.

"Hello Daniel," Anna greeted, a streak of shyness overcoming her again, reminiscent of her childhood.

"Hello," he replied, his approving gaze resting on her as time stood still.

"Father, Nellie," she introduced, "This is Daniel, the newspaper reporter for the Seattle Post Intelligencer I told you about. Daniel, this is my father, Stephen Bailey, and my older sister, Nellie, and her beau, Samuel, a student from father's seminary classes."

"It is nice to meet you sir," Daniel said, as he gave her father a hearty handshake.

He offered his hand to Samuel who appeared reluctant to shake, but finally did. As Daniel acknowledged Nellie, Anna saw a startled look flit across his face. She wondered what it meant and why Nellie did not give him the common courtesy of a smile.

"Daniel, so good to finally meet you," her father said. "Anna has been so busy with her suffrage work and I with my classes, that I have not seen much of her. I understand you have been a great help to her endeavors."

"Thank you, sir. Your daughter is a wonderful gal." His glance toward her revealed a new light in his eyes and she grew warm thinking of his obvious regard.

"I am wondering, sir, if you would give me permission to take Anna on a picnic on the school grounds across the street. My sister packed a delicious lunch for me to share with Anna if it is all right with her, and with you. I would like to celebrate her success this day."

"My boy," her father said while clasping his shoulder, "you already know my daughter has her own mind. If she wants to go on a picnic, she has my hearty approval!"

Anna's thoughts warred within, but only for a moment. The hope in Daniel's eyes was her undoing. "Yes, I would be pleased to go on a picnic with you. Maybe we can talk about the magazine article I want to write tonight."

Daniel's eyes dimmed in response and his smile did not quite reach his eyes. She realized her mistake. "Or maybe we can just celebrate.

Together."

His smile grew, lighting up his whole face. Yes, things between them were shifting.

Her heart fluttered as she wondered what lay ahead.

*   *   *

The church had cleared while Anna was in conversation with Daniel and her family.

She walked between the two white posts supporting the covered entrance, and Daniel gently clasped her arm as they descended the stairs.

Susan stood by the walkway holding a wicker picnic basket and a worn quilt blanket. The humor in her eyes, and the closeness between her and her brother was reflected in the way she playfully pushed the basket against her brother's chest. "What took so long? I wondered if I would have to start eating this myself."

Anna and Daniel glanced at one another and Anna said, "You are welcome to join us."

"No, I don't know if I'd be that welcome." She grinned at her brother. "Besides, mother and I have plans to visit Esther and her family today."

Daniel took the basket and blanket and nodded. "Thank you, Susan."

Across the street from the church stood Alexander Hall, built in 1896 as a school funded by the Free Methodist denomination. Anna's father started teaching there four years earlier to help with basic education of their students. They had added grades each year until they could begin a seminary for young men.

She had spent many hours on the campus and was intimately familiar with the walking path she and Daniel took past the Hall, winding through some woods, and opening up to a small pond, complete with a weeping willow tree to shade them from the afternoon sun. A few mallard ducks swam by, slow and carefree, completing the picturesque scene.

Daniel put down the basket and tried to spread the blanket out by flapping it in the wind. Each time, the fabric landed as a partial rumpled mess, and Anna laughed. He grinned and handed the resistant quilt to her. "Think you can do better?"

"No, I think we can do better together." The words slipped out before she realized the deeper implication of them. His eyes widened as she handed him two corners and their fingers accidentally touched. She wondered at the rapid pounding of her heart. "Here. Hold tight."

She stepped back. The space between them calmed her. She held the other two corners and shook the blanket so it billowed out and he followed her lead as they laid the tamed cover gently on the ground.

"Perfect," she said.

"No, not yet."

"What do you mean?"

"Sit down right there." Daniel pointed to a corner of the blanket.

She sat and spread out her black skirt, careful to smooth away any wrinkles, and to ensure that not even her ankles showed. How providential her clothing was appropriate for both church and this unexpected picnic.

He placed the basket near her and sat beside her.

"And now?" she asked.

"Now, it is truly perfect."

They both smiled.

They laughed, talked, and enjoyed the picnic meal Daniel's sister had prepared. They spoke of Anna's speech from the morning and the angle Daniel would take when he wrote about today's event. Anna told him she planned to write an article that very evening for the magazine, *Harper's Weekly*, based on her experiences with the suffrage movement.

With a wistful yearning, she said, "I hope you will be able to cover *all* the events we are planning, especially the big rally a few days prior to the vote. We'll use music to draw a crowd and speakers to win them over. I'm envisioning a large grand event."

Daniel smiled warmly. "You can count on me being there."

His confident words reassured her, and as the afternoon quickly passed, she wondered at the friendship forming between them. She felt she had known him forever.

Daniel sat for a moment, and her face grew warm as he seemed to study her.

"You were so natural speaking in front of all those people. I believe you were meant to speak and to write."

She shook her head and closed her eyes. "Not everyone has encouraged me the way you have."

"What do you mean?"

Anna considered the sincerity on his face. *Maybe I can trust him.*

She took a deep breath. "In my last year of high school my dream was to attend college to study journalism, but I needed an academic scholarship in order to do so. I tested for it through my schoolmaster. I was consistently at the top of my class. Many hours of testing, and answers were jumping from my mind to the paper with no hesitation. There was no question I had done my best, and in doing so, I'd done the best out of the other students. Benjamin, my beau, was my only real competition, but there were two scholarships to be awarded so I was not concerned."

"What happened?" Daniel leaned forward with interest.

"Our teacher." She swallowed hard. "My completed test was torn in half and discarded in the waste basket. My test had not been sent in for grading. I confronted Mr. Hargrove. He did not believe women should go to college. In fact, he thought my keen mind to be a cosmic mistake."

Daniel shook his head. "You must have been angry."

"There is more," she continued. "While having words with Mr. Hargrove, I realized Benjamin was leaning against the door listening. I expected his support, for him to express outrage at how I'd been treated. Instead, he snickered and said, "*I guess I'll be the top student now.*" He walked off without another word. I was betrayed by my teacher and by Benjamin. How could I be such a poor judge of character?"

Daniel, with head down, was quiet for a moment. "Has any good come from this?"

"Some. Not long after graduation we moved here for a fresh start. My father taught me himself to compensate for what he was unable to provide in paying for college. I've learned much under his guidance and I do not regret the close relationship we have forged. Eventually, I began writing again and turned my direction to magazine publications. I'm still wounded by the betrayal though."

A troubled look passed over Daniel's face. "Some things are hard to let go, especially when life turns your world upside down."

"You sound like you understand."

"Well, I do understand being cheated by a powerful, condescending man."

Anna waited in silence for him to continue.

"I—I grew up on a farm on the outskirts of Seattle." He studied the brightly colored plaid quilt, not meeting her gaze. "My early childhood was happy. Father worked hard and I wanted to be just like him. I fed the chickens, collected eggs, and helped him whenever he asked. We raised vegetables and father had apple orchards."

Anna smiled. "Go on."

"Susan and I still had time to play. We even tried to ride our billy goat, pretending he was a horse. Only once. He hopped in the air and threw me off. Shortest ride I ever had."

She chuckled. "Growing up on a farm sounds wonderful. What happened?"

Daniel shook his head and focused on the pond.

"At first, we'd pack the wagon with baskets of produce and drive to a huge warehouse near the waterfront. The buyer would record what we brought to sell, they would shake hands, and my father would hum all the way home."

"As weeks passed," he continued, "my father grew quiet during those trips. Finally, he argued with the buyer and demanded to be paid the value of his crops. The man laughed, peeled off a few bills, and placed them in my father's outstretched hand. My father held his tongue, but his jaw tightened, and I thought he might deck the man. We had been cheated and we never returned to the warehouse again. My father worked hard, but he started drinking. He and my mother argued. Susan and I would hide in the barn to get away from the yelling."

Daniel rubbed his temple, then gave Anna a sad smile.

Anna's eyes teared up against her will. *How good of him to share his hardship with me.*

He traced the quilting on the blanket's worn fabric and gripped the edge as he continued. "One day the man from the warehouse knocked on the door. His presence meant trouble. He handed my father papers and told him we had thirty minutes to move out of the house. He was now the legal owner of the property including the house, the land, the farm equipment, and all our livestock. We were allowed to take only our personal possessions."

Daniel winced. "My mother ran from the room in tears and Susan and I held onto each other and cried. The man also stated we no longer owned our wagon or the horses. My father hauled off and punched him in the face, knocking him onto his back on our front porch.

"He said, '*You may be able to take my farm, but we are using the wagon and horses to move our belongings.*' My father's dignity was barely salvaged with the small victory of moving our possessions with our wagon."

"This must have been so hard on all of you. Who was the man?"

Daniel blew out a deep breath. His stoic facial expression was betrayed by the low raspy tone as he spit out, "Morgan."

Anna's face heated up, flushed with anger. "No wonder you have such strong disregard for the man."

Daniel tightened his grip on the edge of the quilt. "Yes, I have good reason. He was the middleman at the warehouse. Morgan and others like him realized they could get away with not giving farmers a fair price for their crops. They sometimes paid little or nothing. My father and others couldn't prove they'd been cheated. Morgan learned we had prime land and a mortgage. Morgan targeted us so he could swoop in like a vulture, buy our mortgage, and sell our property to the railroad for a huge profit."

"I cannot believe he got away with this."

"Me neither, but apparently, he grew rich at the farmers' expense until Pike's Place Market was built to help farmers sell directly to customers. Using the market cut out the middleman, but came too late for many families, including mine."

"What did you do then?"

"We moved into town and my father took odd jobs, but he never found his footing in city life. His drinking took its toll and he made foolish mistakes, like gambling to get us out of our small, crowded apartment. My mother became the strong one: taking in laundry, assisting at a seamstress shop two days a week, and selling her home-baked goods to customers she gained throughout the neighborhood. Because of the hardships and poverty, I've vowed never to allow my family to return to such circumstances again. That's why I'm so determined to succeed at my career."

Anna nodded. "So, what happened with your father?"

"He became ill, lingered a long time, and then died. We had grieved for him while he was still alive, so we had no tears left. My mother provided for our family, became strong through adversity, and passed those traits on to both my sister and to me. That's probably why I admire strong women. Like you."

"Thank you." She glanced at him with a shy smile. "I do not think of myself as strong."

"But you are."

No one had ever spoken such encouraging words to her besides her father. She ached over Daniel's hardships, but she admired his determination, his kindness, and his love for his family.

Time stopped when he looked at her with such honest openness. *Where is this headed?* She admired the world around her. *The sky is bluer, the sun is brighter, and the birds' songs are a symphony.* She had never experienced this erratic awkward pounding of her heart with anyone else, not even her my old beau. *I—I could see a future with Daniel.*

Wonderful, handsome, true-blue Daniel.

CHAPTER 6

Daniel hummed while sitting at his office desk and he realized he'd written Anna's name in beautiful cursive on his notepad. He glanced around, but his fellow reporters, including Henry, were busy typing, writing, and talking with sources. Her dreamy face floated before him and a blissful peace settled over him as he thought back to their picnic lunch.

Even sharing his hardships hadn't dampened their time together. He could almost envision spending his life with her, but then the bleakness of the obstacles stood before him, and he couldn't see how God could work this out. He and his family struggled to make ends meet. Adding another support would undermine their precarious financial state, and he would never let the poverty of his childhood happen to any of his loved ones again.

And then he remembered. Nellie. Another obstacle. When he recognized her at church, he could not bring himself to tell Anna what he knew about her sister and ruin what had turned out to be a perfect day. But tell her he must. He would finish his work early and pay her a visit this afternoon.

"Daniel, my office. Now."

Shaw's booming voice broke into his thoughts. Daniel grabbed his notepad and pen and quickly entered the editor's office.

"Have a seat, son." He gestured to the chair across the desk from him. "I'll cut right to the chase. I have some bad news for you."

"What, sir?"

"I'm afraid I have to discontinue the series of suffrage articles you've been writing."

"But, sir."

Mr. Shaw held up his hand to stop him. "No. There is no other way. You do top notch work, but we're experiencing pushback from influential people, including those who pay good money for advertising in our paper. I was afraid this might happen. We can't afford to lose them to the competition."

"I understand." His voice low, his body slumped in the seat.

"Don't let this discourage you, Daniel. We all experience setbacks. You have a keen sense for reporting, so don't let your emotions muddle your judgement."

Daniel nodded and then remembered. "What about my article on Miss Bailey's talk at church yesterday?"

"I liked your angle. We are running the article on the religion page."

"But, sir." His voice rose and Daniel was ready to argue the point.

Mr. Shaw held up his hand again. "Hear me out. The piece won't draw the same kind of attention a front-page story would, but we may find some sympathetic readers who might consider the suffrage movement in a whole new light once they read your article."

He settled back down, more relaxed and willing to concede for the moment. "I see your point. It could be beneficial. What assignments will you be giving me now?"

"Well, you're not going to like this." Shaw placed his elbows on his desk and rubbed his hands together. "I need you to cover the anti-suffrage angle of the movement."

"But—"

"Sorry, my boy. We're in a bind. An influential man pressured me to fire you, but I appeased him by offering your writing about the opposition."

"How can I write something against my beliefs?"

"I'm sorry, Daniel. A good reporter will write objectively. The best will write convincingly on a view opposed to their own. Either do as you're assigned, or I have to let you go."

Daniel steeled himself against the sickening sensation churning his stomach, not wanting to disclose how his dreams were crumbling with Mr. Shaw's every word. "I can't imagine doing this."

"You are a clever man, Daniel. You'll figure it out." Mr. Shaw cleared his throat and looked down. "There's something else as well."

"Yes, sir?"

"You can't help out on any more public suffrage events. You must maintain a neutral appearance for the newspaper's sake."

"Mr. Shaw!"

Shaw held up his hand. "I have no choice, so you have no choice. If you must be present at the rally, fine, but no helping or interfering, not if you want to keep your job *and* your career in the newspaper business. Do you understand?"

"Yes, I understand." Defeated, Daniel stood to leave, a foreboding force squeezing his chest. "Just tell me this. Was James Morgan the one who pressured you?"

"I'm not at liberty to say, but you do know the man. I cannot officially put you on any story concerning our illustrious city leaders, but I would be downright disappointed if the investigator in you didn't see a story here. Maybe nothing is published in the paper until someone is caught in the act and put away. If you get my drift."

Daniel noticed the weariness and the creases in Mr. Shaw's face. When had he aged? "I will do my best, sir."

"I know you will, son. Be careful. I am counting on you."

"Thank you, sir." As Daniel closed the office door, he realized how much Mr. Shaw had come to mean to him. He worked hard for Shaw's approval, not just to advance his own career, but because he genuinely cared for the man who had been a father figure to him.

In the meantime, he'd think about Shaw's

cryptic words and determine how to follow up on real leads. His goal was to find a different way to support Anna and the suffrage movement, and not jeopardize his career. The idea of having to choose between them was unthinkable, but he couldn't afford to throw away all he'd worked so hard to achieve. He dreaded telling her about the edict from his boss, and to disclose what he knew about Nellie. Then it occurred to him that he could use his reassignment as an opportunity to learn the other side's tactics, even if he did have to put a positive spin on their activities.

Meanwhile, spending time with Anna to enjoy her company warred with all the bad news he would need to tell her. Maybe they could take an evening stroll. A moonlit walk might soften his words, and the thought of seeing her again brought a smile to his face as he tried to focus on his work.

*   *   *

Anna hurried to the corner just as the electric streetcar arrived. She paid her token and replayed what had happened as they poked along Seattle's busy streets. James Morgan's house. How? She had been tutoring his niece for several months, but wouldn't have known that fact if Mrs. Jorgenson hadn't asked her to tutor Clara at their home while she recovered from an illness. Mrs. Jorgenson had never mentioned Morgan was her brother, and now she could no longer work with Clara.

She hadn't realized how attached she'd become to the loving little girl. She would truly miss her, but more to the point, she did not have an income and because of the uproar when Morgan barged in, she had forgotten to ask Mrs. Jorgenson for recommendations. She pressed down on her legs to stop the trembling of her limbs. How far could Mr. Morgan reach into her life and the lives of those she loved?

The streetcar passed Frederick & Nelson's and she mused at the popularity of their new tearoom which employed some forty waitresses dressed as French maids who sold pastries at each table. The store had grown to take over a whole city block. Due to the construction boom after the Great Fire and the large number of people who had drifted here beginning with the Klondike gold rush, Second Avenue was now the center of the business district. She scrutinized the businesses with new eyes, wondering if she should try to get work in one of them. The Bon Marche had recently opened. Named after the owner's favorite store in Paris, Mr. Nordhoff boasted the department store to be the largest on the Pacific coast.

She'd also heard the salmon cannery was hiring women, but the canneries were close to the dark side of town; streets filled with businesses featuring gambling, saloons, and brothels. She shuddered at the thought of those who'd been forced into dismal work due to unfortunate circumstances and wondered if suffrage could help them. Regardless, the work offered was not what she wanted. She wanted to write, to be published, to use her mind and be paid for creative thought. Her dream had changed from journalism like Daniel's profession, to something more in-depth, but was it even possible?

The streetcar came to a stop in front of the post office, and she hopped off, pulled the envelope from her handbag, and sent a prayer heavenward as she dropped the precious work through the mail slot, to begin its journey to the editor of *Harper's Weekly*. She'd stayed up half the night writing and revising what she considered a compelling article about the inside workings of the suffrage movement. If they published this, her message would have a national audience.

Anna startled at the sound of noisy drums, chanting, and boisterous voices from down the street. Curious, she walked toward the commotion, accompanied by other onlookers. First, she saw a large banner with the words, *"Votes for Women; Never!"*

Then she saw familiar flaming red hair among the women. Traffic stopped as she watched her sister pass by alongside other anti-suffrage marchers, including James Morgan.

Nellie turned her face away when she saw Anna, but Mr. Morgan cast her a triumphant smirk. The wind knocked out of her, Anna struggled to breathe, and her whole body trembled from the shock of seeing Nellie here.

How could Nellie do this?

Her vision blurred as tears welled up in her eyes. She wiped them away with her embroidered handkerchief, but the floodgates were now open.

Why didn't she tell me she was so opposed to suffrage? Maybe Samuel had influenced her. And did father know and not tell me?

I will talk to Daniel. She had planned to stop at the Seattle Post Intelligencer office anyway, but now she had to share before she burst, and it had to be with Daniel. He would know what to do.

*   *   *

Daniel was writing the key points of his anti-suffrage story when a shadow fell across his desk. Standing in front of him was his angel-faced Anna, except, her face was flushed, her eyes red, and there was no smile to be found.

He sat upright, searching her tear-filled eyes, and laid down his pen. He wondered if she was upset about his article from yesterday's edition. His editor had removed all references to James Morgan and the fiasco involving the sabotage of the pies. He dreaded telling her about his latest assignment. "What's wrong?"

"Everything."

"Here, sit down and tell me what happened." He handed her his handkerchief which she gladly accepted, dabbed her eyes, and gripped it hard in her hand.

"I—I got fired from my tutor job by Mr. Morgan."

"Mr. Morgan?"

"I was tutoring his niece, but I didn't know the connection. We usually meet at my home, but Clara had been sick, and I went to her house for the first time today. I discovered it was Morgan's house when I arrived, but Mrs. Jorgenson assured me her brother would be gone for the day. Unfortunately, Mr. Morgan returned to retrieve forgotten papers, saw me, and in a rage, fired me. I had planned to ask Mrs. Jorgenson to refer me to her friends for more students but in the confusion I forgot."

Daniel, sickened by the thought of how Morgan had hurt Anna, struggled to find words of comfort. "I'm so sorry, Anna."

She barely nodded in response, hiding her face behind the rumpled handkerchief.

He sat in silence waiting, listening, wanting to reach out and touch her arm or take her hand for reassurance, but he stopped himself. He was in no position to think of her as he wanted, and yet—

Sniffles subsided and she composed herself, the pain still evident in her eyes. "I mailed my magazine article at the post office."

He nodded, unsure of her continued downcast appearance. "Good to hear."

"Yes, the best part of my strife-filled day." Her sorrowful face made him suspect there must be more to her story.

"Did something else happen?"

"Yes. After I mailed my article, I heard a loud commotion. A large group of people were marching against suffrage. James Morgan was there, which did not surprise me. But you will never guess who else was there, helping to carry a banner."

Daniel had a lump in his throat and swallowed hard. He tried to prepare for what he was sure was coming. "Who?"

"My own sister. I cannot believe she would be involved, nor hide this information from me. Did she really believe I would not find out?"

The walls of the office pressed in on him, and a sudden stifling heat made it hard to breathe. "Maybe she didn't want to hurt your feelings or cause an argument."

"I think she should have trusted me, trusted our relationship enough to not hide this."

Daniel felt smaller than the mouse which lived in the hole by the floor molding ten feet from his desk. In fact, the mouse was lucky. The small furry creature could safely hide in his hole. He could not. He kept his focus on the pencil he was fumbling with, wanting to avoid the intensity of her gaze. "I have a confession to make."

"What is it, Daniel?"

"When I met your sister yesterday, I thought she looked familiar. I realized I'd seen her at one of the opposition rallies. I believe she's even pictured in one of the photos we published last week on the front page."

He pulled a newspaper from his desk drawer and handed the evidence to her. "Here. Take a look."

She studied the photo for a moment. "It is Nellie. I could not find this day's paper to read, and when I asked Nellie, she told me she wrapped spoiled meat in its pages. I thought it odd at the time."

Daniel nodded, still fingering the pencil.

Anna dropped the paper on the desk and her eyebrow arched in question. "You *knew* and did not tell me?"

Daniel's stomach knotted together like tangled

yarn. "I—I didn't mean to keep anything from you. We were having such a nice time on our picnic I didn't want to spoil our day. I had no intention of keeping it from you. I am so sorry."

Daniel held his breath as Anna sat in silence. Typewriters clattered around them, reporters rushed by to beat deadlines with breaking stories, and loud co-workers used their voices to get their points across. All of this became a dull roar as he waited, scarcely daring to breathe, hoping he hadn't slammed the door on something precious with Anna.

Her face softened. "I forgive you, but, please, make sure you do not keep things from me."

"Agreed." Daniel relaxed. "I understand. Thank you. Here, a peace offering courtesy of my mother."

He handed her a slice of gingerbread from the generous portion he'd been given before leaving the house. "I have something else to tell you."

Anna tilted her head to the side, the same eyebrow raised in a quizzical arch. "Oh?"

"My editor changed his mind about publishing the series of articles on the suffrage movement. He's receiving pushback from influential community leaders. He plans to print today's article on your talk at church, but I'm afraid this will be the last one unless something huge happens."

Disappointment clouded Anna's face once more. "Are you sure you cannot get him to change his mind?"

"No. It's worse than that. I have to write an anti-suffrage piece to give their point of view."

Her eyes narrowed as she flashed him a look of

disbelief. "Why can't you refuse? Have the editor give the assignment to someone else."

"Look. I tried, but I'm bound to do as my boss requests." He grabbed her hand. "There's more."

"What?"

"I have to appear neutral on this issue." He swallowed the lump in his throat. "I cannot help you with your events or give any appearance of support in public."

"How can your boss dictate what you do on your own time?"

Daniel shook his head. "I know. He shouldn't, but he's feeling pressured by powerful people. I'm sorry, but if I'm not careful, I will lose my job. For my family's sake, I must choose my battles wisely."

She pulled her hand away, and glanced down, dejection apparent. This had not been a good day for either of them.

"I—I do understand, but what will I do?" Her eyes clouded over, worry extinguishing the bright expressive lights. "I must find ways to get the word out."

"You will. There will be ways I can help behind the scenes. And, I'll still attend your big rally before the vote. I can be there to write a neutral story, but I'll be cheering you on in my heart."

"Thank you. It gives me comfort to hear that."

"Excuse me, Daniel." Henry stood with a note in his hand. "I hate to interrupt you two lovebirds, but Shaw got a call and this message is for you." He handed it to Daniel. "Sounds urgent."

As Henry left, Daniel opened the note and read the message. A wave of weakness rolled through his body.

"Daniel, what's wrong? Your face is pale."

Anna took the message Daniel handed to her and read aloud, *"Daniel, something terrible has happened to our shop. Mother and I are upset, but we are not hurt. Please come as soon as possible."*

"I have to go."

Anna touched his arm. "Let me go with you," she pleaded.

He paused, scrutinizing her eyes, clear blue pools of compassion. Any hesitation he had vanished. "Yes, let's catch the next streetcar."

Grabbing his overcoat, he left his desk in disarray, relieved to have Anna by his side, even as he wondered what they would find. The dress shop was his mother and sisters' only hope for financial independence. And his hope to one day have a family of his own. Daniel's fledgling dream of marrying Anna seemed to fly further away with every passing moment.

CHAPTER 7

Daniel and Anna arrived by streetcar to 4th Avenue. Daniel forced himself to walk a slower pace so Anna could keep up as they hurried to check on Susan and his mother. He saw their sign, *The Wright Dress Shoppe*, in prominent letters as they drew closer. Nothing seemed amiss at first glance, but then he saw the remains of the shattered large pane glass window.

He quickened to almost a run, his insides roiling as fearful thoughts assailed him.

Fragments of glass littered the sidewalk, large, fractured pieces were prominent on the display floor, and ice-like crystals shimmered in the sunlight, embedded in the stylish evening dress which had been featured. The door was open, and his sister's attention was on the push broom she wielded to take care of the shattered remnants.

"Susan." She set the broom aside and Daniel opened his arms to embrace her. "Are you and

Mother all right?" He searched her face for the truth.

"Yes, just unnerved. She's in the back, resting."

She shook her head like she still didn't believe this had happened. Her stoic expression, with darkened eyes and washed-out skin, told him she was not all right.

He took the broom. "Your face is pale. "Sit down while I sweep."

"Thank you." Her weary voice betrayed the smile she wore. "Still watching out for me."

The weak quip from his sister did him good. *She still remembers.* The past was hard to examine. He pushed the thoughts away by saying, "We will always watch out for each other."

Anna stepped forward, took Susan's arm, and led her to a high back red velvet chair. "I am so sorry. Can I get you some water while I check on your mother?"

"Thank you. I would be grateful." Her smile trembled a bit. "Fortunately, we were in the back fitting a customer, and there was no one else in the store. Otherwise, well, I am sure someone would have been hurt."

Mrs. Wright stepped out of the back room. "No need to check on me, dear. I am fine."

She brought a glass of water to Susan, appearing no worse for wear. Once again, Daniel admired her resilience.

"There's my strong mother." His eyes teared as he wrapped her in a protective hug. He wondered if she really was fine when she did not let him go. *When had her hair streaked gray?* He needed to be more attentive to her. The thought of her aging brought a lump to his throat. She finally loosened her hold and they stepped apart.

He searched her face for answers. "How did this happen?"

His mother walked over to the counter where the cash register stood and picked up a baseball-sized rock and a piece of paper with scrawled writing attached.

Daniel lifted the rock from her hand. A flash of anger streaked through him like lightning. "Well, that would do the job."

Placing the stone back on the counter he held out his hand and read the note aloud. *"Stop this suffrage nonsense. Or else!"*

"Clearly a warning, then." Daniel squeezed his eyes shut. He wanted to deny the danger his family was in, but the concrete proof tore away any vestiges of safety his mind had retained. "Did you see anyone?"

"No, we did not," Susan said. "A gentleman stopped in to check on us. He was on his way to the bank and heard the glass break. He mentioned a man hurrying away in the opposite direction but did not get a good look at him."

"Did you get this man's information?"

Susan sighed. "No, Daniel. We were so shaken, the thought never crossed our minds. I'm sorry."

"It's all right. I have some contacts. I'll get to the bottom of this."

Anna and his mother disappeared into the back while Susan and Daniel cleaned up the floor and the sidewalk. From the back room, he called the police to come and file a report, and a glass replacement business to take care of the large, shattered window.

He returned to the front of the shop, surprised to see a customer perusing woolen skirts and dark colored fabrics, oblivious to the damage. When the dark-haired woman turned around, he puzzled at the big grin on her face. His mother and sister stood nearby smiling as if they had a well-guarded secret.

"Do I know you, miss?"

"I certainly hope so, but all the better if you don't recognize me."

"Anna?" The long tresses of dark brown hair were partly hidden by a fashionable hat, decorated with ostrich feathers, and her navy-blue jacket and skirt gave her the air of a business woman like his sister. "What is this?"

"I'm going undercover to assist you, thanks to your sister's and mother's help."

Susan stepped forward. "We can disguise ourselves as well. We want to help catch this scoundrel."

His mother nodded in agreement, the sparkle back in her eyes.

Clearly outnumbered, he saw the problem if he didn't reign in his family's plan. "Listen, it would be highly suspicious if all of you were to be in disguise. I need you to carry on with business as usual, act as lookouts, and visit with your customers, innocently gathering information to solve this crime."

"Anna, you and I will go right now and try to track down an informant. I would like you to stay out of this, but I would rather you were with me instead of acting on your own."

Her eyes danced at his words. "You know me too well. Yes, let's go while the trail is still—what do they say? Hot?"

He smiled and took her arm. "Yes, that's what they say."

He regarded his mother and Susan. How could he protect them? "Please be careful. Report anything suspicious, but be discreet about what you do. And call if you need me."

He couldn't shake the thought that the trail would lead directly to James Morgan.

*　　*　　*

Their quest of locating an informant today hadn't yielded any results, but Daniel had shown Anna behind the scenes techniques of investigative reporting. They spoke with a few of his contacts but none were willing to talk. He'd passed Anna off as a reporter in training. There were a few raised eyebrows, but he was relieved her disguise protected her identity. They'd done what they could, and he left her with the promise that he'd let her know when he set up a meeting.

Meanwhile, she'd hurried home to have a long overdue talk with Nellie. He hoped the two sisters would work out their differences. He would do anything to remove the pained confusion from her lovely eyes.

Daniel had to admit it. Spending time with Anna, even on an investigative case, was good for his soul. He knew Anna was the girl for him.

Everything about her, from fire and passion to empathy and sensitivity, spoke to him with a resonance unknown before in his life. She was his soulmate. Surely God would work out the details of how they could be together.

So much for his own plans.

*   *   *

Anna slipped down the hall past the kitchen and up the stairs to her bedroom without anyone noticing. She didn't want to explain to Nellie or Ruby why she was in disguise. Besides, since Nellie had a connection with Mr. Morgan, she couldn't take any chances on Nellie discovering their investigation into the vandalism at the dress shop. As she returned downstairs, she set these thoughts aside, determined to have a real talk with Nellie.

"Dinner smells good. What's cooking?" Anna asked as she entered the kitchen.

"Stew," Nellie replied, using a wooden spoon to stir the hearty vegetables and beef in the cast iron pot on the stove. Nellie kept her stiff, impenetrable back to Anna.

"We need to talk." Anna approached Nellie and put her arm loosely around her waist.

"I do not believe we have anything to talk about."

Anna dropped her arm to her side. "Yes. Yes, we do. We both know I saw you at the opposition rally walking with James Morgan. Why would you not tell me you felt so strongly about this issue?"

Nellie turned and glared. "You would not have

accepted my decision. You were so jubilant about your involvement with suffrage that you were not listening to what I had to say. You dismissed me like I knew nothing about the subject. And at the same time, you are practically preaching for women to make up their own minds about these things. What if all women do not agree with you?"

Nellie's angry words were like a slap in the face. She had never considered her sister might be so passionate in the opposite direction of her own beliefs. "How could I even know this when you have not spoken a word to me?"

"I was trying to keep peace in the family. We have always been close, and I did not want to ruin what we have." Nellie put the lid back on the pot. "Maybe father and Samuel were right. I should have told you rather than letting you find out the way you did."

"Father knew and did not tell me?" She winced at the thought of her family's deception. *Why does everyone keep things from me? First Jonathan, and now Daniel, and her own family.*

Anna placed her hands on her hips. "We are family. We should not be keeping secrets, even if they are painful to share."

"You may be right." Nellie sat down at the Victorian style dining table.

Anna sat across from her and thought the table symbolic of the growing barrier between them. "You mentioned Samuel. Does he hold the same views as you? Or did he influence you?"

Nellie covered her mouth with her hand and avoided Anna's gaze.

"Please, look at me."

When Nellie glanced at Anna, her guilty expression revealed the truth. "He is strongly opposed to the suffrage movement, then?"

"Yes. As a seminary student, a pastor in training, he believes we need to protect the home, the family above all else. I agree with him. If women vote they may develop other independent notions about work."

"Are you really so passionate about your view?"

"I think I am. I see both sides, but I want to support Samuel and his work in the areas we hold in common."

The front door opened. "Come on little one. Let's have you take a snooze. Go on up the stairs. I will be there in a moment."

The sound of Ruby's voice and small feet on the stairs soothed Anna's troubled soul. Having a friend who believed strongly in the same cause was good medicine. *What a shame I cannot count on Nellie in the same way.*

"Good afternoon." Ruby's cheerful voice resonated through the kitchen. She smiled for just a moment. "Did I interrupt something serious?"

"We're fine." Anna glanced at Nellie. "We were about finished."

"All right. I'm putting Emily down for a short nap before the rally. That will give me time to dust and clean in Mr. Bailey's study before he returns home."

"Thank you, Ruby," Anna said. Ruby nodded at both sisters and left the room. Anna heard her humming as she climbed the stairs to tuck in Emily.

"You have a rally this afternoon?" Nellie asked.

"Yes. We decided to schedule later in the day when the men are leaving work to give them the opportunity to hear some speakers." She sipped her now cold tea. "Maybe you would like to come too?"

Nellie raised her eyebrows in surprise. "I—I am not sure. What time does your rally start?"

"Four o'clock. In front of the newspaper office. I don't want to pressure you, but maybe hearing their views would be helpful."

"I will consider attending. I do need to take care of a few errands so if I come, I will meet you there."

Nellie and Anna both stood at the same time. Nellie's manner was stiff, uncomfortable. Anna sought Nellie's gaze and although Nellie smiled for a moment, the wall between them still existed.

Anna made one last attempt. "Thank you for talking with me. I hope we can be honest with one another."

"It is worth a try," Nellie conceded.

Nellie rushed from the house and Anna puzzled over the strange interaction they'd had. *Maybe I'm reading too much into her behavior. I still feel like she is keeping something from me.*

She shook her head at the mystery, gathered up what they needed for the event, and shortly after, she, Ruby, and Emily left the house to continue marching toward the right to vote.

CHAPTER 8

Daniel watched from his office window as the women gathered on the sidewalk and organized for their rally. He glanced at the clock, straightened his tie, and grabbed his jacket and notepad. "Henry, I'm gone for the day. Got a contact to meet."

Henry grunted and Daniel took the stairs two at a time to get to Anna prior to the march.

"Anna, hello."

"Hello. Did you change your mind?" Her quizzical bright eyes seemed to appraise him as she tried to hand him a sign.

He smiled, appreciating her passion for the cause, but he shook his head. "No. I am sorry. You know I can't help. I thought I'd say hello and let you know I'm meeting a contact."

Her head bent slightly, disappointment clouded her eyes. "Oh, I thought you would wait so I could come with you."

"I know." His heart sank, not wanting to let her down again. He placed a loose strand of her hair behind her ear. He was close enough to catch the subtle scent of lavender. "I don't have a choice. Much of my day was spent finishing up the anti-suffrage article, and this is the only time I could schedule to meet. I'll let you know if I find out something useful."

She gave him a sad smile and shook her head. "I still cannot believe you have to write *that* article."

"I know." The silence between them was palpable. He sighed. "I've got to go."

As he walked away, he glanced back to see she'd resumed her role as leader, handing out signs and giving instructions. The kindness, intelligence, and inner strength she shared with others each day only increased his admiration. How lucky he was to have a gal like Anna. And yet, he pushed away the thought of being forced to choose between her and providing for his family.

Thirty minutes later he was still in the back of an eatery, one *not* owned by Morgan. He warmed his hands with a cup of coffee, waiting for his contact to show up. Finally, his informant, the man he trusted to provide critical accurate information for many of his news stories, slipped quietly in the booth across from him, a fisherman's cap partly covering his eyes, and a few days of salt and pepper beard growth which made even Daniel believe the man had just returned from sea. He was solid. He knew things about people he just shouldn't. He wondered what the man knew about *his* life.

Both men nodded.

"Let's get to the point," Daniel said. "Do you know if Morgan is behind the vandalism and threats toward pro-suffrage businesses?"

Wyatt leaned forward. "I'm a businessman first."

He noticed Wyatt's outstretched palm and Daniel drew a few crisp bills from his wallet, glanced around, and placed them in his hand.

Wyatt grinned and pocketed the money. "Now, where were we?"

"I asked about Morgan's involvement."

"What isn't he involved in?" Wyatt chuckled and lowered his voice to a near whisper. "The trouble is proving your suspicions. He uses enough other people to keep his own hands from getting dirty. And if caught, they're too afraid to implicate him, so they take the rap themselves."

"Tell me something I do not already know."

"Morgan's man, Jed, was seen fleeing the area of your family's dress shop after the vandalism."

"Thank you. I suspected as much."

"There's more."

"Go on."

He looked around, then continued. "Word is, there's someone new involved. Someone close to those you love."

*   *   *

Anna's excitement about the day's march was tempered by the frenzied butterflies unsettling her stomach, and a growing uneasiness about Daniel; his acceptance of his anti-suffrage writing assignment, his boss's mandate not to appear to support suffrage, and not including her when meeting his contact. No matter. She was working with those she'd come to regard as sisters and friends. That's what was important right now. She smiled at Miss Betty, the older woman who had misunderstood their discussion about goals and goats at their first women's club meeting. Esther held onto Miss Betty as they lined up for the march. Susan stood arm in arm with Ruby who held little Emily's hand, but no sign of Nellie.

"Ladies, it's time!" Anna blew a whistle and a few stragglers fell into place. She sang. *"I'll overcome some day, I'll overcome some day."* The sound of their united voices soared skyward. *"If in my heart I do not yield, I'll overcome some day."*

They marched one city block before turning the corner to head toward a park.

Ahead of them a wall of people lined up to block their path, carrying signs and shouting horrible names at them. Angry men, most likely workers from Morgan's businesses and others he had influenced, stood like a formidable force, with a smattering of women in their midst.

Anna gasped. "Oh no!"

Her ladies faltered, and she swallowed the thick lump in her throat. She held her sign higher and walked toward the crowd. She blew her whistle over the sounds of their opposition. Police stood at the storefronts, arms crossed. She could not count on them.

The suffragettes drew within ten feet of the unruly men. Her breath caught as she saw Nellie's red hair glistening in the sunlight. *How could she?* Their gaze locked for a moment before Nellie looked away. Samuel stood by her side. With contorted face and neck veins popping, he shook his fist, and yelled at Anna and her ladies.

Bullies. Big bullies shouting down women who only wanted a voice. Daniel should have been here. *Why isn't he here when I need him?*

She did not want to endanger her women. They were at an impasse. She would turn them around and they would march away with their heads held high. Efforts thwarted, they would live to fight another day.

Whap! Something hit Ruby and splattered down the front of her dress. A rotten tomato.

Crack! Ouch. Anna's chest was hit by something hard, no, runny. Raw egg oozed down her blouse. She glanced up in time to dodge another projectile aimed at her.

Samuel and the other men laughed as they continued to lob objects. Nellie stood there frozen for a moment, then yelled at Samuel to stop.

Her heart pounded as the urge to flee coursed through her body. Anna shouted, "Run!"

The women reacted on cue. They took cover behind light poles, by the storefronts, and even hid behind a few idle police officers. Finally, the police stepped in, blew their whistles, pulled out their clubs, and yelled at the offenders to break up the melee and go home.

"A little late, are you not?" Anna remarked to a sandy haired officer sporting a well-trimmed mustache with long twisted ends.

He smirked and walked away. However, Nellie ran to her side.

"I am so sorry." Nellie's eyes glistened, sincere remorse in her voice. "Anna, let me help you, Ruby, and Emily get home."

Anna glanced around at the other women. "Let me check on everyone and then, yes, we will go home together."

Once they were back at the house, Nellie drew baths for all three of them, and helped them settle into their night clothes early. Other than a slight purple bruise on Anna's chest, everyone was physically fine, but a little shaken. They rested together in the living room, crocheted blankets covering their laps, while they sipped cups of hot chamomile tea Nellie had brewed.

Nellie's usually bright blue eyes were dimmed. "I feel responsible for what happened. Samuel instructed me to tell him about any events you had planned, but I never expected he would do anything like this."

Anna looked into her sister's eyes. "You could not have known."

"Well, I do now. He slinked away after he hit you and the other ladies. I know he hit what he aimed at because he bragged about how good he is at throwing a baseball." She shook her head. "He wanted to hurt you. My own sister. We are finished. Our courtship is off."

Surprised by the depth of her own regret, she studied Nellie's face. "I am so sorry, Nellie, but are you sure? You have worked so hard at securing this relationship with Samuel. You seemed so happy and full of hope. I do not want to be the cause of discord between you."

"You are not. And do not be sorry. I am not even sad." She held a hairbrush, stepped behind Anna, and gently brushed her soft strawberry curls, as they used to do when they were younger. "I am more upset with myself for not seeing his true colors earlier. If his devotion to a cause gives him permission to hurt innocent people, then he is not the man for me."

Ruby held a drowsy little girl in her lap. "I admire you, Nellie. Samuel does not deserve you."

"I agree," Anna said. "I am so happy we are no longer at odds. I can accept you have a different opinion about women voting, but we can still respect one another."

"Thank you, sister." Nellie smiled, walked over to the table, and brought the morning newspaper to Anna. "I know you didn't have time to read this morning. Neither did I. This might be a good time to catch up."

"Oh yes." Anna thumbed through the paper and came to the editorial page. She gasped and let the paper fall to her lap.

"What's wrong?" Ruby asked. "Your face is white as a cotton sheet."

Anna couldn't speak, shock coursing through her body.

Nellie let go of Anna's hair, placed the brush on a side table, and picked up the fallen paper. She read the title aloud. *"Why Women Should Not Vote."* Her eyes widened. "By Daniel Wright."

*　　*　　*

Daniel replayed the conversation with his informant as he hurried back to the rally to find Anna. His concern for both Anna and his family created momentary indecision on who he should check on first. He decided to find Anna and Susan and bring them with him to check on his mother.

He bounded from the streetcar and rounded the corner and saw...street sweepers. The rally was over already? He didn't have time to waste. Someone in their midst was a traitor and he had to discover their identity in order to protect his family. At least with the rally over, he didn't need to worry about Anna. She would be safely home by now.

When Daniel reached *The Wright Dress Shoppe*, the closed sign hung prominently in the window. Perturbed by the unlocked door, he opened it slowly, on guard for what he might find. He picked up a brass table lamp for protection and called in a tentative voice, "Mother, are you here?"

"In the back." She came to the doorway of her alterations room, a measuring tape hung around her neck and her reading glasses low over her nose. "Daniel, what are you doing with my lamp? My goodness, you will have me searching for monsters under my bed."

"Did you know your door was unlocked?" He did not mean to sound so stern. He locked the door, and glanced down the momentarily deserted street, returned the lamp to the table, and met his mother at the door of the alterations room.

"It's all right, Daniel. My last customer just left.

I was basting a hem before locking up."

"You need to be more vigilant, Mother. Someone broke the Belle Bakery's window two blocks from here. We have to be prepared for more trouble. I do not like you here alone, especially this time of day."

He was on edge, fighting a foreboding darkness, and he paced in front of his mother as he tried to shake it off.

"Daniel, you have not acted this way since you were a boy. You don't have to worry. We will be fine."

Crash! Daniel instinctively hunched over his mother to protect her as their newly replaced window shattered into tiny flying fragments. Shaken, but unhurt, they ran to the front of the shop as a man wearing a black derby hat crossed the street and hurried away.

"Stay here." Daniel jerked the door open and bounded after the dark-clothed man who now ran at full speed.

Daniel crossed the street, dodged two carriages, and gained on him. The man slipped into an alleyway and Daniel chased him as the man entered an abandoned building. Daniel stepped into the darkened building and stopped to let his eyes adjust to the diffused light from the smoky dust-encased windows.

A noise to his right drew his attention. He turned as the man in black brought a length of metal pipe down toward his head. Adrenaline surged through his body. His heart nearly beat out of his chest as he recognized he was in a fight for his life.

Daniel roared as he grabbed onto the cold lead pipe and pushed against his attacker as the two struggled for advantage. He used the full weight of his body to push the taller man backwards. As their bodies shifted, the light illuminated the man's enraged face.

Daniel gasped. "Samuel!"

The man's crazed eyes, darkened countenance, and curled lips sent a wave of fear through him. The apparition no longer resembled Samuel.

Samuel bellowed an anguished cry as he pushed him away, letting go of the pipe. Daniel stumbled backwards over debris and fell.

By the time he picked himself up, Nellie's beau was gone.

*   *   *

Anna's throat closed tight. Could there be an explanation? But then, she recalled his change in behavior. First, he quit covering the suffrage events, he was eager to not stay for today's march, and now this—this newspaper opinion piece with his name boldly emblazed as the byline. This opinion piece was much worse than an objective article showing the other side's views. Was their relationship all a charade to obtain the next big story? Was his career too important to let anything or anyone get in his way? Have I been wrong about him, just like I was about Benjamin?

Urgent pounding interrupted her thoughts. *What now?* Nellie and Father stood behind her as she tightened the belt on her robe and opened the door.

"Daniel." His suit jacket was torn, covered with grime, and his dirt-splattered tie was askew. His rumpled hair was accompanied by a red scratch down the right side of his face and a puffy cheek.

"Were you in a fight?"

"Yes, but I'm fine. I need to warn you about Samuel. He's not who he seems."

Determined to keep a civil tongue, even as her heart was breaking, Anna replied, "Well, I'm wondering the same about you."

"What do you mean?"

Nellie handed Anna the newspaper and she pushed the offensive publication into Daniel's chest, harder than intended. "This is what I mean."

She watched as he unfolded the paper and read the headline. His face paled. "Anna, I know how this looks, but there's been a mistake. Let me explain."

She crossed her arms. "It seems self-explanatory to me."

Daniel looked at Anna's father and sister. "Mr. Bailey, may I speak with your daughter alone?"

"Certainly, my boy. I'm sure you two can work this out." He placed his hand on Nellie's shoulder. "Let's go into the kitchen, dear."

Anna gestured toward the couch, and they sat on opposite ends. Daniel's shoulders sagged as he leaned forward, head down. "Anna, some of this is my writing, but other parts are not." He raised his eyes. They begged for understanding. "My words have been twisted. Nothing like this has ever happened before. You have to believe me."

Her stomach churned, sickened by the

conflicting emotions competing for preeminence. After what had happened with Benjamin, should she believe him? "I want to believe you. This is such a shock."

"I'm sure it is, but I'm afraid I have more bad news."

Anna braced herself for the next tidal wave. "Does it have to do with your disheveled appearance?"

"Yes. I caught Samuel breaking the window at my mother's shop. We fought, but he got away. You need to know in case he tries to make contact."

"I wish I were surprised, but he was an agitator at our march today. I wore one of his tomatoes home."

Daniel's eyes grew wide in astonishment, then burned bright with the protective look of a warrior, and finally, softened to concern.

"I'm fine, but I was shaken."

"I'm so sorry. I turned his name into the police so I doubt we'll see him around."

She nodded.

"Anna, I'm concerned for my family. I do believe Morgan is behind this, but until he's implicated, I have to step further back from *any* association with the suffrage movement. Mother's sales have dropped since the vandalism, and now we have the repair costs for two windows. I'll talk to my editor about what happened to my article, but I feel I'm putting my mother and sister's safety at risk, as well as our livelihood with my involvement. I'm going to ask Susan to step back from suffrage events as well. My boss prefers I stay away from the final rally. He plans to be there with a few other reporters. The pressure on the newspaper is tremendous, and I have to be careful about what I do and say. I hope you understand."

Anna felt like the floor had just dropped out beneath her feet. Was there no one willing to stand up for her, to care enough to sacrifice on her behalf? Benjamin had not been willing, and now, neither was Daniel. She cared for him, and she thought he cared for her, so why should it be this way?

"I do understand it's a risk, but if we win, all those fears could be laid to rest. I had hoped—" *You had promised to be there.*

Daniel's earnest eyes caught her own. "What did you hope?"

She shook her head. "It doesn't matter now. You protect your family. *And your career.* I will see suffrage through to the finish line."

He nodded. "I am sorry. I've been put in a really bad position."

His eyes revealed his pain and conflict, but there was no more to be said. "I think I'd better go."

"Yes, that would be best."

"Anna, I hope you know—this is just temporary. After the vote—"

She stiffened, unable to think ahead, unable to explain further. "Yes, after the vote we will talk."

She walked him to the door, careful to maintain her composure until he was gone. Tears spilled down her cheeks as she passed her worried family and ran to her bedroom. She sobbed into her pillow until her reddened eyes were nearly glued shut. She could not see how this could be made right. Was

Daniel no better than Benjamin?

How will I ever bear up? I—I truly love him. A mind-numbing dizziness overtook her.

What would she do about the final rally? She and several other women were slated to speak. Should she find someone to take her place? No, she would not succumb to self-pity, nor would she let personal troubles interfere with the mission she'd been given. She would stay strong and run the race to the finish line.

And she would not think about Mr. Daniel Wright.

CHAPTER 9

Daniel paced the living room and jingled his keys in his pockets while his mother read the morning newspaper and Susan packed for the rally. He glanced at his sister. "I don't think you should go."

"I have to be there." Placing her hands on her hips, Susan said, "We won't beat that dead horse again. And, frankly, boss or no boss, I'm surprised you would let anyone or anything stop you from being by Anna's side."

He stopped his pacing and sat on the edge of the sofa. "There's nowhere else in the world I'd rather be."

What a scalawag he was, abandoning Anna just when she needed him most. Why did he have to make a choice between those he loved? He should be able to protect them all.

His mother set down the newspaper and smiled. "Daniel, this is wonderful. Not only did your boss apologize for using your byline, but he stated that you're a man of integrity, reason, and incredible ability, devoted to your job and the people of our community. Your opinion piece published the same day will clear up any misconceptions."

"Yes, Mr. Shaw was gracious in his apology and his tribute," Daniel said. "He was also dead set on giving me my own opinion commentary to make amends. We're still investigating who tampered with my write up. Interesting coincidence. Today's paper also reports Samuel Knapp's arrest for the vandalism of your shop and other pro-suffrage businesses in the Queen Anne neighborhood. To mention the suffrage movement may create sympathy to give women the vote."

"I agree. Listen to this part," Mother said. "Mr. Knapp was wanted for questioning, but evaded police for five days until caught as a stow-away on a ship headed for San Francisco."

He nodded. "Morgan's influence may be wearing thin if he couldn't get Knapp out of town. Samuel will talk and expose Morgan's dealings. Meanwhile, Mother, you haven't yet said what you think of my opinion piece. Of my views on suffrage."

"I am a little uncomfortable that you mentioned Susan and myself."

He walked over to his mother. "I hope you understand why. I cannot imagine braver or stronger women than you and Susan. The same qualities of perseverance, courage, and dedication you live by are what I admire in Anna as well. Because of you, I'm unwilling to give up on her so easily."

His mother's kind eyes appraised him. Softly, she said, "Is that not what you're doing? You take too much on yourself. Do what you can, do what is right, but leave the results in God's hands. Truth will win the day."

Her words were like a message to him straight from God. *Is this where I've gone wrong?* Memories flashed through his mind; fearfully hiding with Susan as their parents fought, angry at his father as his mother struggled to keep them fed, and now, carrying the weight of providing for them long after the women in his family had become self-sufficient. He loved God, but had he trusted Him? This was the missing piece, the stumbling block which kept him stuck in the past and burdened by a load God never meant for him to carry. *Lord, forgive me. Please take my burdens and help me trust you beyond what my eyes can see.*

His mother cocked her head. "Daniel, are you alright?"

He smiled wholeheartedly. "Yes, I'm as right as a ship bound for sea." The oppressive weight was gone. With a lightness in his step, he recognized the change and reveled in his newfound freedom.

"See you at the rally." He quickly kissed his mother on the cheek, grabbed his coat off the rack, and opened the door. "Please say a prayer for me."

Daniel arrived while the stage was being set up. He had an urge to help, but kept his distance as the men worked. Surely, if he kept in the background, his editor would have no qualms, especially after allowing him to run his opinion piece.

"Daniel? What are you doing here?"

"Henry, I'll just be a bystander. I need to be here for Anna."

The skeptical look in Henry's eyes was not lost on him.

"I know how it looks, but I can be here and silently cheer her on."

"The boss will be here too." Henry slapped him on the back. "Make sure you don't cross the line."

"I'll do my best."

Henry grunted as he walked toward the stage. He joined another reporter and their editor, Mr. Shaw, who looked toward him after a brief conversation, and shook his head. Fortunately, more people had arrived, milling around, and filling the space between them. He saw several of Anna's suffragette friends, but no sign of her or Ruby yet. What could be keeping her?

*   *   *

Anna and Ruby hurriedly packed signs and banners for the downtown rally. This was their last opportunity to convince voters to support women's suffrage. Ominous gray clouds threatened a downpour which could drown their last hope of getting the word out, but Anna couldn't think of that now. They were running late.

As she walked down the hall, Nellie stepped in front of her, blocked her path, and waved a newspaper in her face. "You must read this."

"Not now. I will read today's paper after we return home."

"No, you *must* read it. Now." Nellie's insistence puzzled her, but she took the paper and read the title, *"Why Women's Suffrage is Vital to our Future,"* by Daniel Wright. Light-headed, she stumbled her way to the dining room table and sat down, almost afraid to read the words. First, she saw a sincere apology written by Daniel's editor, who had used Daniel's byline on an article pieced together by others that included *some* of Daniel's writing. Then, he praised Daniel for being a man of integrity—a quality she once thought was true of him.

Her heart beat faster as she read Daniel's column. He wrote of a hopeful future if women could vote. This was based on the strength, perseverance, courage, and love of the women he knew like his mother and his sister. His words rang true, much of the content in line with the speech she would deliver today at the rally. By the time she finished reading, her face was wet with tears. How could she have doubted him?

Then, she knew. She'd let her past wounds dictate who she was and how she acted for far too long. The past had reared its ugly head to destroy her future. *Lord, heal me. Help me let go of my past once and for all.* Daniel was nothing like Benjamin!

Nellie smiled sympathetically.

"Thank you," Anna said.

Nellie said, "You know, I think I will come to the rally today, to support you."

"I would be pleased to have you with us," Anna said.

Ruby and little Emily were standing nearby,

smiling. "Here, here," Ruby said. "Let's go. And maybe you'll have a chance to see Daniel."

The twinkle in Ruby's eyes told Anna their conversation had been overheard. Hope surged as they hurried to the rally.

*   *   *

An enthusiastic crowd gathered while the ladies put the finishing touches on decorating the platform constructed for today's rally. A band played familiar patriotic music, drawing passersby, while balloons and streamers in red, white, and blue added significance to the event. She wondered if the flyers her ladies had distributed were responsible for the swelling numbers of their crowd. Perhaps the tide was turning in support for their cause.

Anticipation built as Anna and other speakers reviewed their speeches, aware not everyone there would be supporters. She was more at ease since Esther had proposed using some funds to hire private security, just in case the police did not step up if needed.

She scanned numerous faces searching for Daniel, but didn't see him. Would he change his mind and be here? She had so much to say her heart was ready to burst.

She forced her thoughts away from Daniel as she listened to her ladies at the podium. Esther's prominence as a doctor's wife would speak to other society women, as well as those who respected her and Dr. Thompson's work in the community. Ruby's story of her missing husband and caring for her daughter alone would resonate with those in precarious financial conditions, or those who feared the same could happen to them.

Well-known suffrage leader, Emma Smith DeVoe, had called Esther saying she hoped to attend the event, but they'd not yet seen her. Anna had heard enough about the controversial woman to want to meet her, but wondered if her appearance would do more harm than good. A few more women spoke, but with shorter speeches to keep the interest of the crowd. So far, the gathering had been respectful, and the crowd applauded politely for each speaker. They even laughed when little Emily yelled out, "That's my mommy," while Ruby spoke.

The sky grew lighter, the clouds softened, and the sun filtered through in places, slivers of light kissing the gathering with a warmth of approval. Anna stepped forward, placed her speech on the podium, and grasped its sides for support. She glanced around, hoping Daniel may have changed his mind and shown up. She did not see him. Shaking away thoughts of him, she focused on her speech. More than anything, she wanted the crowd to hear the reasoning, to understand for themselves, and make a decision based on the truth she shared.

"We are your daughters, your sisters, your wives, and your mothers. We strive to gain women the vote, not because we desire to leave our homes and communities, but because we want to improve our homes and communities."

Anna panned the crowd as they applauded, and out of the corner of her eye to her right, she saw movement toward her. *Daniel!* Their gaze met and he touched the brim of his fedora as he nodded, a widening smile on his face. She returned his smile. Her renewed hope for a future including Daniel was not in vain.

"If our voice is important in the running of our households and the raising of our children, should not our voice be important in the influences allowed to grow within our neighborhoods? Should we not be concerned with the unfettered proliferation of gambling, saloons, and other unseemly establishments? Should we not wonder about the quality of education our children are receiving? Should we not have a say in creating more parks for families to enjoy when our city is rapidly growing? And finally, should we not work to ensure the existence of respectable decent paying jobs for women should something happen to the provider in our families?"

Enthusiastic applause again gave her a moment to view her surroundings. The growing crowd was alive, clapping and raising their *Right to Vote* signs up and down. Truly, for the first time in her life, there were others who recognized the rightness of a woman, like her, using her mind. The validation of her abilities broke open the guarded places, the hidden wounds rinsed clean not by man, but by what she perceived as a God-given gift. Like a lightning flash, she recognized she was healed.

With her spirit soaring, she glanced at her notes, not wanting her personal triumph to interfere with what she still needed to share. As she looked at the expectant crowd, a movement to her left caught her eye. She gasped as she saw James Morgan and his men working their way to the front. His scowl left no doubt he was not pleased.

"Your words are all lies!" he yelled. "Go home now!"

His men joined in, yelling, "Go home now! Go home now!"

Suddenly, Daniel appeared at Anna's side. His protective stance reassured her.

"Men, stop. These women have earned the right to speak. No one is compelling you to stay at this rally, but if you are here to disrupt it, security will forcibly remove you."

At these words, Morgan paused, then signaled to his men, who dispersed into the crowd. Anna caught sight of Daniel's boss, shaking his head toward Daniel. *Oh, Daniel, what have you done?* She turned to thank him, but he was gone.

She returned to her notes to continue her speech. Morgan would be even more incensed when he heard the next part. She swallowed hard and took a sip of water. *Lord, help me.*

"We have opposition to gaining the right to vote, mostly from those in powerful positions who are afraid of losing control and losing money. They have used fear as a tactic to undermine our efforts. You have an opportunity to vote not only for women's suffrage, but to vote against an individual running for city council who promotes many of the schemes we are concerned about as a community. Some here have unduly influenced those in businesses and have corrupted many in government as well. Were we to elect one such individual to the Seattle City Council, his power over others would grow, and our ability to have a voice concerning our community will diminish. The choice is in your hands."

She was almost afraid to find Morgan in the crowd, but there he was, standing below her in the center of the front row, his hate-filled eyes staring at her like the devil himself. She had thought herself safe, part of a large group of people in a public park and hired security standing by. Had she underestimated what Morgan was capable of doing? The hair at the nape of her neck prickled as he formed a gun with his hand and pretended to pull the trigger.

Bang, he mouthed. She watched Daniel quickly work his way over to Morgan. She hoped he would be there in case the threat was real, but her heart beat wildly as she worried about her safety and Daniel's. God could not have brought her this far to have an ignoble end. *Could He?* The applause stopped and the crowd waited in anticipation.

Anna cleared her throat. "We—we ask you to rise above the fear, consider our city and its potential, and ask how we can be our best selves, our best neighborhoods, our best communities. There is a time for us to speak out, to be outspoken about what truly matters to us. Is not this a form of love in itself, a kind of outspoken love, not meant to aggrandize self, but meant to give ourselves away for those we love, not only for our family and community, but for generations to come? Let us love well."

Applause thundered from the crowd, the band played, and the ladies on the platform hugged in celebration, and a commotion broke out in the front row.

Dread washed over Anna as she saw the melee erupt directly in front of her. She clutched the podium as Daniel and James Morgan fought, no, wrestled, and those nearby moved away from the brawl. They separated. Morgan pulled a handgun, pointed it at Daniel, then at the security guards. Morgan turned his head. Daniel charged and grabbed Morgan's arm. They fought for control. Daniel forced Morgan's arm straight up as a stray shot fired.

At the sound of gunfire, Anna's ear-piercing scream echoed through the park. She watched the scene in horror, unable to move.

Daniel pushed Morgan off balance. Both men fell to the ground and struggled once more for the gun. Daniel knocked the weapon away, but Morgan crawled on his hands and knees toward the weapon. Daniel pursued Morgan, but held his side in obvious pain.

"Help! Police. Help!" Anna yelled while Daniel struggled to grab onto Morgan's leg. For Anna, time stood still while visions of Daniel laughing during their picnic, asking her to dinner with hope in his eyes, his support of her speaking and working for women's suffrage, and the first time they had met— when he had shown such gentle care as he lifted her and Ruby out of the mud.

I cannot lose him now. Not after all we have been through. I love him. I really love him.

If she had to intercede herself, she would. She hurried down the wooden steps, but whistles blew as police and hired security surrounded Morgan. Daniel backed away on his hands and knees before rising, and Anna stopped short of the police.

In handcuffs, Morgan was screaming at the officers. "Don't you know who I am? I am James Morgan! I can make or break you. Let me go."

As the officers took him away, he passed by Anna. "You think you can get away with defamation of my character? You will be hearing from my lawyer, especially since you just cost me my election."

Anna straightened to her full height. "Sir, if you need to find the one responsible for the direction your life has taken, just look in the mirror."

She turned from Mr. Morgan and ran to Daniel, breathless as her heart raced and her body trembled. She would not be kept from him for one moment longer.

As she drew closer, she noticed his dirty clothes were torn, his tie askew, and his face darkened by a mix of dirt, bruises, and blood. He held his right side in pain. She touched his arm lightly, dismayed by his appearance.

She was afraid to ask, and it took all the strength of propriety to not take him into her arms to comfort him. "Are you hurt?"

Despite his wounds, his eyes danced as his gaze connected with hers. "Nothing unable to heal, especially if you're with me."

She nodded. "You looked like this the last time I saw you."

Daniel chuckled and moved closer to her. "Yes, I may need my tailor to supply me with more durable suits."

"Or you could stop getting in brawls."

"Oh no, fair maiden," he said as he grinned and placed his right hand over his heart as in a pledge. "I will always defend home and hearth, at least in as much as God directs me and gives me strength."

She smiled, joy swelling inside like lit fireworks. "I welcome your words more than you can know."

"Anna." Esther Thompson hurried toward her accompanied by a well-dressed matronly woman in her early sixties whom Anna did not recognize. "I'm so glad I found you. I want to introduce you to Emma Smith DeVoe. She traveled from Tacoma to hear you speak. Are you both all right?"

"Yes, we're fine," Anna said, as she glanced at Daniel. "Or, we will be now."

He mouthed to her, *we will talk soon*, as he backed away, holding his side as he left.

She did not want him to leave, but she gave him a smile in response and turned to the two women. "Mrs. DeVoe, I am so pleased to meet you. I have enjoyed reading about the gentle womanly strategies you use to gain support for suffrage."

"Well, Miss Bailey, thank you. Your speech touched me deeply and I am encouraged for our future generations. With young women like you, delivering reasoned arguments and not acting on our feelings alone, our words will eventually be taken more seriously, and will make a lasting impact.

"Thank you, Mrs. DeVoe." Anna kept her composure, but her mind was on fire with ideas for speaking and writing. To receive encouragement from a woman of such importance affirmed her calling. Her world had been jarred wide-open. Youthful dreams once snuffed out, had been reborn. "Your words are too kind."

The older woman patted Anna's arm and smiled as they regarded one another. "No, I should be kinder. Like you. I will always remember you."

CHAPTER 10

Several months had passed and the volume of chatter at dinner kept rising as the Wrights and Baileys, as well as Ruby, competed to share their experiences voting for the first time. Nellie had prepared a celebration meal of pot roast, potatoes and gravy, carrots, and homemade bread, but it sat mostly untouched as all continued to speak. Even though Nellie had not voted today, Daniel noticed she had caught the excitement of the momentous change this represented.

"Please, let's have more orderly conversation." Anna's father tapped on his glass with his knife. "I would like each one to share what's transpired, and to recognize our blessings."

"A wonderful plan, Father. I am thankful to vote for the first time in my life," Anna said. "To write my name and cast my vote, and know I have a say. And consider the irony, James Morgan should be sentenced for his crimes this very same week."

Daniel hung on Anna's every word, inspired by her tenacity, enthusiasm, and purpose. She was his very breath. His gaze held hers as he said, "Yes. The jury returned within one hour of hearing the case. To be found guilty of attempted murder, bribery, and money laundering, not to mention his petty crimes. He'll be sent away for a long time."

She continued to search his face, for what? A declaration? She already held his heart in her hands. Didn't she know? Thankfully she'd not given up on him these past months, waiting as he quietly considered how to provide for her, as his *wife*.

Daniel's insides roiled under her continued scrutiny, as if she were trying to read his thoughts. He grew warm as she watched him, and wished she'd speak again so he could hear the voice of the woman he admired, no, loved, wholeheartedly. He was torn, undecided about the most important decisions of his life. When should he announce his news? And, when should he ask Anna for her hand in marriage?

Ruby spoke up, diverting his thoughts. "I—I do feel for Morgan's sister. What will she do without her brother's support?"

Susan straightened in her chair. "Oh, we have good news. Dress orders have increased dramatically, so Mother and I are expanding our dress shop into the vacant space next door, and we need to hire extra help."

Daniel raised his glass of water as for a toast. "I am so proud of both of you for all your hard work and determination. But, are you saying you are hiring Mrs. Jorgenson?

"Yes, exactly." Susan's words wore a triumphant ring, but Daniel puzzled over the decision.

"What kind of work can she do?" Daniel asked as he helped himself to more bread.

"We didn't know," Susan replied, "Mrs. Jorgenson is a skilled seamstress. Her brother thought it beneath her to have a job, so he supported her and Clara, and she'd planned to move out once Clara was grown."

"Such wonderful news," Anna said, her voice as enthused as if she'd given Mrs. Jorgenson the position herself.

"But there's more." Susan paused a moment for dramatic effect.

The table of family and friends expectantly waited, except for Emily who hummed and busily soaked her bread with gravy.

Susan's mysterious smile plus her conspiratorial wink at Anna piqued Daniel's curiosity. "Secretly, Mrs. Jorgenson has been seeing a Mr. Caldwell, a logging supervisor who lost his wife two years ago in a runaway carriage accident. He's a kind, well-respected man who has proposed marriage. They didn't know how her brother would take the news, but Mrs. Jorgenson reported her brother to be much relieved she'd made a match, and he gave his blessing. There is a touch of humanity in the man after all."

Ruby cried out, "What wonderful news. I've felt so badly for her and little Clara."

"How fortunate for Mrs. Jorgenson," Daniel said. "I am a little surprised Morgan thought enough of his sister to see this was for the best."

"We can pray he will find forgiveness," Mr. Bailey said. "And for Samuel as well."

He turned a regretful look to Nellie. "My dear, I am sorry I didn't see his character flaws. His scholarly approach to his studies, his dedication, and his passion blinded me to his deficits, which apparently, are legion."

"This is not your fault, Father. I pray his two-year sentence will redeem him, but he knows there's no future for us. Better to care for our household than to be married to such a man."

Daniel observed Nellie's peace and her thankfulness for the narrow escape from life with one so ill-suited and admired the resilience of the Bailcy family.

As Anna glanced at Ruby, Daniel noticed concern flash over his beloved's face. Then, he saw Ruby's dimmed eyes, and wondered if she was thinking about her husband. How difficult it must be to celebrate under such uncertainty.

Their dinner nearly done, Anna and Nellie cleared the table for dessert, a nice apple crisp with cream. They'd only taken a few bites when they were interrupted by a heavy knocking on the front door.

"I will be back," Nellie said. "Please, keep eating."

*   *   *

Nellie returned, a curious look on her face as she perused the mail. "This looks important."

She gave an official large envelope to Anna. *Is this another rejection letter?* Anna opened the large heavy envelope. With everyone watching, she prepared herself for another letdown. She scanned the cover letter.

"I—I'm going to be published!" She could scarcely believe the written words on the page.

"Read it aloud," Susan said, her voice rising above the rest of the group's well wishes.

Susan's mother nodded and leaned forward. "Yes. Please."

"All right, then." Anna glanced around and held the letter to the fading light from the window. "Dear Miss Bailey, after reading your article and seeing suffrage has passed in the state of Washington, we contacted Mrs. Emma Smith DeVoe to verify your involvement. Based on her glowing endorsement of your leadership, your character, and the exciting drama surrounding how you successfully dealt with opposition to your campaign, we not only want to pay to publish your article, we would like to sign you for a series of follow up articles as well. Our editor will contact you with further details once we receive your signed contract. If you have any questions please call at the telephone number listed above. Sincerely Yours, J. H. Abbot, Chief Editor, *Harpers Weekly*.

"Congratulations, Anna." Daniel's deep voice, warm with affection, resonated through her being. He shot her a look which conveyed how proud he was of her accomplishment, but he scrutinized her as if searching for something deeper. He did not appear to be himself tonight.

"We have a bright future," Daniel said, as he lifted his glass of milk as if to toast.

We? Anna wondered. Apparently, the others wondered too as they all had smiles, giggles, and questions in their eyes.

"Well, I—I mean, I have news too." His face flushed. "I—I got a promotion at the newspaper. In a matter of months, I have gone from being in danger of losing my job to becoming Mr. Shaw's new assistant editor."

"Oh, Daniel! How wonderful." Anna's heart leapt. Could this be what he had been waiting for? They'd been courting for months, and yet, Daniel had been silent about his feelings or the possibilities of a future together.

His mother gave his arm a squeeze. "I knew your time would come."

"Great news, son." Mr. Bailey gave Daniel a pat on the back. "This surely is a good day."

Nellie cleared her throat. "The excitement may not be over yet. We have one more letter, addressed to Ruby Olson."

She held out the lone missive to Ruby who stared at the envelope before slowly taking it. All eyes on her, she carefully opened the letter and with shaking hands, pulled the paper out. Handwritten words flowed over the water-stained pages. She read to herself while Anna and the others watched.

Ruby caught a cry in her throat, placed her hand over her mouth, and began sobbing as she handed the letter to Anna. Emily hugged her mother, patting her back to give comfort.

Anna scanned the letter, fearing the worst, but

said, "Peter. He's alive."

"Thank the good Lord," her father said. "I have prayed for the young man for months."

Anna nodded. "We all have."

Smiles, laughter, and praises followed, but little Emily's face showed bewilderment. "Mommy, why is everyone else happy when you're crying?"

"We're all happy, dear. For me, these are happy tears. Your papa is coming home." A smile lit up the faces of both mother and daughter.

"Oh Mommy! Happy tears are lovely." She hugged her mother's neck and Anna's eyes pooled with tears of their own. Happy tears *were* lovely.

Then the questions started. But how? Where was he? Why has he not contacted you until now? Is he hurt? When will he return? Anna held up her hand to silence everyone. She glanced at Ruby who nodded and held her daughter close.

Anna explained, "When Peter and his crew were fishing in the Pacific, they put into port in Astoria to sell their fish and gather new supplies. While there, they were shanghaied— knocked unconscious, dropped into a boat through a trap-door at a saloon, and forced to serve as crew on a larger vessel far out at sea. They eventually gained the trust of the captain and when they put into port at San Francisco a week ago, they weren't heavily guarded, which allowed Peter and his crew to escape. They scraped together some money and plan to be home by train in a few days."

Nellie took her seat and shook her head. "If we have any more good news today, I shall surely faint!" Sounds of laughter and feelings of relief and pure joy permeated the lively group.

When Anna glanced out the window at the brilliant sky and the setting sun, she wondered if she and Daniel would have any time alone before the end of the evening. A melancholy sadness set in, but she noticed Daniel smiling at her and she nodded.

"Anna, would you accompany me on a walk before the sun sets."

"Yes, I'd be happy to."

Her melancholy chased away by a growing hope, a cautious expectation, she wrapped up warm against the waning winter chill in her fur collared gray wool coat, and Daniel held open the door leading into the yard. The glass-like water of the bay and the snow-covered mountains were muted reflections of the fiery reds and oranges of a hand-painted sky. The sun was like a glowing orb casting off its remaining embers before returning to its earthen hideaway. The glories of the artistry took Anna's breath away. For this moment in time, there was no one on earth but her and Daniel.

She trembled, but not from the cold. Their breath as vapors, mingled as they stood in silence at the choreography of the beauty enveloping them. Aware of Daniel's presence, strength, and character, she embraced the moment. He turned to face her with his face full of soul and fire as he took her hands and got down on one knee. She had waited so long. Was this really happening?

"Anna, I love you with all my heart and I cannot imagine life without you. I would shout my love for you with the same kind of outspoken love you have expressed so well. I will love you all of my days. Please, Miss Anna Bailey, will you marry me?"

Anna could scarcely believe her ears. Because of life's uncertainties she had tried to guard her heart, but she had failed, and she was glad. Never again would she doubt Daniel's sincerity or his love for her. He knew her and he loved her.

"Yes, oh a thousand times yes." She pulled gently on his arm, and he stood into her embrace. "I will declare, Daniel, my love for you, a love without bounds," she whispered into his ear.

"Love makes for the finest poetry." he whispered back. "And I intend to woo you all of our days."

Daniel leaned over and found her lips, and the sweetness of their kiss filled her soul. Just as the final flames of the sunset burst across the sky, her feelings for Daniel soared and she knew without a doubt their love was a deep abiding love. Their love would see them through their life together—a life filled with adventure, hardships, and joy. Much joy.

"We should go back inside, my love. Tell our families," he whispered.

"As long as you stand behind Nellie, my dear."

He gave her a questioning look.

"To catch her when she faints."

Daniel laughed as he grabbed her waist and held tight. "I'm not sure they believed this day would come. We may need to catch them all."

Jeri Stockdale is a member of the Northwest Christian Writers Association and American Christian Fiction Writers. Her first novella, *Christmas Gone Awry*, was published in the book, *Christmas of Hope: An Anthology of 7 Christian Inspirational Holiday Stories* in October 2016.

Born and raised on the Kitsap Peninsula in Washington State, Jeri has fond memories of family outings to the beach and tromping around in the woods with her dad as he surveyed land for sale. This instilled a love of nature and animals which is reflected in her writing and her life, but it was when she met Jesus as a child, that she understood the gift of being caretakers of God's creation. She's travelled to several states, enjoying their distinct beauty and cultural differences, and has developed a love of history through these experiences.

Since those early years she's received a business degree, worked as a management analyst, and home schooled her three children to adulthood. Her life experiences have influenced her to write inspirational women's fiction, romance, and historical fiction stories. When not writing, she enjoys time with her family and working with a discipleship ministry at her church. She shares her home with a menagerie of pets including dogs, cats, and horses. Jeri also enjoys gardening, nature walks, small towns, and researching family history.

www.jeristockdale.com

www.facebook.com\jeri.stockdale

Author's Note

Dear Friends,

Thank you for spending your precious time with me on a brief excursion into Seattle's past. Born and raised in the Puget Sound region, I have fond memories of riding the ferry to Seattle with my family, and visiting the waterfront and the Ye Olde Curiosity Shop, Pike's Place Market, and the iconic stores in downtown. I became interested in Seattle's history and delving into its role in the suffrage movement.

Like my main character, Anna, I often felt my voice was silenced or my words weren't given the validation they would have received if I'd been a man. Her struggles are similar to my struggles, and to those of many women who want to be heard. My story, set in 1910, the year voting rights for women were passed in Washington State, became a beautiful way to explore those issues and to work through how God would have us to live and to give through an outspoken love.

As children, we learned to be quiet and to just do as we're told. As women, we often find ourselves in a similar role within our families or church or in the workplace. Even today. Society's norms have pushed against our efforts to live the calling God has given us. Sometimes we're squelched by society's dictates, or even by those closest to us. With the Holy Spirit calling us to Himself and His mission, have we lived a lesser life than that which He had planned?

Outspoken Love offers one such story. A young talented woman has been stifled in her attempt to live the gifts that God has placed within her, in spite of the encouragement and teaching of her kind, loving father. As she's placed in a leadership role, she grows in her ability to speak out, not just for herself, but on behalf of others. Through this, she learns to take a stand for what's right, and finds that in actively loving others she's also loving herself, and becoming more fully who Christ intended her to be.

My hope is that my story will fan into flames God's work within each of us. Every person has value and a voice that needs to be heard. As the conduit of His message of hope, love, and grace, we need to encourage others to find their voices and use them for His glory. And as Anna discovers, we never know where that may lead. By being obedient to His call, God will do a transformational work within our own hearts. My story is an historical romance, but it's also a picture of God's journey within each of us.

Thank you for traveling this road with me. You can find more information at www.jeristockdale.com , including signing up for my newsletter, or find me on Book Bub and my

face book author page. I would love to hear from you! And I hope you'll join me for the second book in *Love's Promises*, called *Gracious Love*.
Blessings,
Jeri Stockdale

Historical Notes

Delving into Seattle's history and its role in the suffrage movement through an historical romance was an opportunity to take a brief look from a Christian perspective at a turning point in our history. Women wanted a more active role in their communities for different reasons, but for many concerned about families, they wanted safe parks and play spaces for children, and childcare for mothers who had to work. Families had been harmed by alcohol, gambling, and bordellos, and women sought to limit the spread of those establishments in their community.

All characters presented in *Outspoken Love* are a figment of my imagination. Except for Emma Smith DeVoe, who served as President of the Washington Equal Suffrage Association (WESA). She was a force for the suffrage movement in South Dakota and Idaho before moving to Washington for her husband's health. Considered a controversial figure by some, due to her heavy-handed leadership style, she actively campaigned for years, accomplishing extraordinary things.

In 1908, the Washington Women's Cookbook was published through the WESA as a way to raise funds for the cause. The cookbook was sold during the 1909-1910 suffrage campaign, including at the Alaska-Yukon-Pacific Exposition in Seattle. Its pages included pro-suffrage quotes as a way to spread their ideas, but the cookbook's subtle message was that giving women the vote could mesh with women still being the keeper of the homes.

Pike's Place Market, an active farmer's market and popular tourist area, was developed to help farmers and other small sellers receive a fair price for their goods, cutting out the middlemen who eventually were paying them less than what it cost to grow their food.

Frederick and Nelson's began in 1890 as a furniture store. They had 28 horse-drawn delivery wagons to bring goods to their customers. In 1903 they opened a popular upscale tea room staffed by 40 waitresses dressed as French maids, who brought a selection of pastries to their customers' tables. By 1906, Frederick and Nelson's encompassed the whole block and offered a selection of ready to wear women's suits and gowns.

I hope you enjoyed these "tidbits" about Seattle's history. There is always so much more unearthed than can be placed in a fiction story, especially a novella. May *Outspoken Love* whet your appetite to learn more, whether it's about Seattle's history, the suffrage movement, or about following God's call on your life. God bless you.

Acknowledgements

Ultimately, I'm thankful to God for His hand in my writing journey. He is the One who opened the doors, gave the opportunities, and provided a loving community of giving writers to help me grow in my knowledge and craft.

A special thanks to Cynthia Hickey and Winged Publications for their work in publishing *Outspoken Love*, and to Darlene Panzera, my mentor, for her tireless effort in keeping me on track. Jacquolyn McMurray, my critique partner, has been that extra set of eyes I needed so often. Kate Breslin is my fellow author and encourager extraordinaire, and Beverly Basile, is my friend and fellow traveler along this road. There are too many others to name, but I do believe I've thought of you all. Thank you for the support from our local Penning on the Peninsula Writers group, as well as those from the Northwest Christian Writers Association and Oregon Christian Writers who have spoken into my life. God is good.

Finally, a special thank you to my family, friends, and prayer partners. I appreciate your encouragement, support, excitement, and prayers. I believe God has brought us together for such a time as this. May we each be His hands, His feet, and His voice to a broken world in need of a Savior. Blessings to you all!

Made in the USA
Monee, IL
03 May 2022